The Sitter

And other Five Minute Stories

by

Sue Cole

The Sitter and Other Five Minute Stories

Cover image by Sue Cole. Clock by Wendy Kershaw

9 781838 085414

To Peggy, for giving me the opportunity.
and Colleen for making it possible.
and Jacky, always.

At the Beginning

He struggled through the shallows to lie on the beach. He took a deep breath of clean, warm, perfumed air as he surveyed the world around him. An expanse of pure white soft sand was ringed with deep verdant greens and the tempting shade of a mangrove. Behind him was the crystalline surface of translucent water washing softly, sparkling in the sun, reflecting the vast canopy of an opaline sky in its gentle crosshatching of the lapping currents.

It had taken aeons to get there, through the water, from the deeps to the shallows, braving the tides, measuring their movement. He had felt himself grow, develop and become something quite different as he did so.

As he lay there, he had a vision. He saw himself moving across the beach, enjoying and perhaps eating the greenery, responding to the scents in the air. He imagined himself with legs, with other beings, with the ability to climb the trees, to take to the air even. In his future he would grow scales, fur, feathers, would become titanic, proliferate in infinite variety: would survive whatever this world could send him.

Perhaps he would even learn to stand on two of those legs, to become the master of his world. He would be able to cross continents, to rule his dominion, to imitate the most complex of other creatures' abilities. One day perhaps he would be able to use the earth's resources for himself, to communicate through the air and spread his beliefs to all.

But there could be problems. If there were too many of those future creatures, they would clash over those resources, would perhaps communicate in ways that were not ideal, attempt to spread their beliefs to others with different beliefs, who might resent such imposition.

1

He also imagined the good times. Enjoying being in a group of like-minded creatures, producing more such creatures with a specially chosen partner, spending time with those of his own choice, relishing this beautiful world, luxuriating in the way he had shaped his environment for himself.

As he lay there, on that untouched beach, under a chemical-free sky and listening to the wash of the unpolluted water, he had a further vision. He imagined himself, in the far distant future, with those he loved, spending time together in such a place. He would lie on the sand, under the shade of the mangroves and run, delighted, to the seductive clarity of the water. He would feel the caress of the current, would release himself into the immanence of being and the peace of contentment. He would be aware of how his body responded to the waves and revelled in the warmth of the sun through the water.

Then he had a revelation. If the best thing in the world was to be in that water, why go through with all of the rest of it? So he turned on the sand and went back into the sea.

The Sitter

It was plain fact. She hated having her picture taken. Her husband, however, wanted a portrait to hang on the stairs with the other family pictures, to show what great relatives he had.

But, for Elizabeth, it was purgatory. She really couldn't explain why, but just the thought of it made her shudder. Perhaps it was that old idea that having a picture taken somehow took some of her soul. That she would lose something of herself, her intensely private self, disturbed her. But it wasn't really that, she was not so unsophisticated that she could genuinely believe such nonsense.

Perhaps it was that she hated the idea that, in years to come, there would be a reminder of how she looked when she was young, an image leering at her as the bloom faded from her skin, her eyes softened, her hair faded and her face sagged and wrinkled. She simply didn't want that hanging over her as she would have to deal with growing older. Again, it really wasn't that. It would maybe be nice to have a reminder of how beautiful she once was.

Then again, it could be that she felt insecure about the pose, that she would look awkward, give a poor account of herself, maybe even give too much of herself away. Again, that wasn't really it. Surely the portrait artist would ensure that her pose was elegant, that her beauty would be properly lighted. Unless she told him otherwise.

She thought, eventually, that it was down simply to the fact that she didn't like being looked at. She hadn't liked the fuss at her wedding, with people looking at her; she didn't like the way the people who followed her husband stared at her, judging and gossiping about their lives. The gossip mongers, the chatterers with nothing else to do, they all looked and stared and

3

commented. That was what she hated, it wasn't the picture at all: it was the exposure. It didn't matter if it was in person or in image.

So, she decided. She would sit for the picture. After all, her husband was a good man, a good husband. He treated her well, gave her presents, fine clothes, reasonable independence and took care of her every need. She would indulge him in this desire, however much she hated the thought of it. But, she would ensure that the picture was somehow not right, that he would not want to show it, that no-one would want to look at it.

Accordingly, she laid her plans. She would ask to be seated in front of the window which looked over the river, telling the man that this was a particularly favourite view of her husband's. She realised that if she sat there, the background to the picture would look odd: she would hide the fall of land which made the horizon line uneven.

She wanted to sit obliquely, so that her features would need to be rendered at an angle. That would make the planes of her face most difficult to capture, especially with the evening light falling. Few artists would be able to carry it off, but the suggestion that this would capture an unusual picture should persuade both her husband and his image maker.

She would wear her plainest clothes. A simple black, smocked dress with a plain scarf. Her hair would be parted in the middle, unadorned and left. She would argue that this would show her face most naturally but she knew that her husband would prefer her to be in her finest garments.

She needed to do something to ensure that her expression would be impossible to capture. A naughty idea suggested itself to her. There was a new lad working in the office; a pretty boy, dark and handsome, from Sicily. His wicked, flirting charm always made her smile. She had no real desires for him other than to look at his beauty. Ironic, really. So she asked him to come to the sitting room when the picture was being taken. She would come up with some excuse. She knew that she wouldn't fail to smile when he came in, and so further affecting the portrait, rendering her expression strange.

Finally, make-up. A pale foundation, a little shading, pale lipstick and some brown shadow in the corner of her eyes would just about do it. The picture would be done, her husband could not complain, but neither he nor the artist would be happy with it.

The picture would disappear, the artist would take it with him. She would not be looked at.

Finally, she was ready. The man came into the room with his paraphernalia.

'Good evening, Mr. Leonardo,' she said, 'please call me Lisa.'

On Southern Region

I settled myself with a cardboard cup of tea and an old favourite Zane Grey novel. The train slid smoothly out of Ramsgate station. As it did so, a man took the seat opposite me, across the table. He placed his wide-brimmed hat on the luggage rack, eased his slimline jacket from his shoulders, adjusted his black bootlace tie and smoothed his slender moustaches. As he chewed on a toothpick, his gold tooth glinted. He took out a well-worn pack of cards.

The train passed the points, the bridges and the old VW factory. As it did so, something whizzed past the window. An arrow. A whoop and the sound of galloping horses signalled the troop of Indian warriors racing the train, as they challenged the iron horse. A grinning face, daubed with paint and with long black hair adorned with feathers looks into the carriage, hand waving a tomahawk in challenge. Six of them, young, handsome, brave. They keep pace with the train, continuing their game of firing arrows at it and grinning threateningly at the passengers.

As the train flies through Minster, the braves melt into the scenery, alert to the sound of distant rifle fire. These riflemen are ruthless; they have something more to gain than prestige. There is gold on the train and they intend to have it. The train slows as it passes Grove Ferry and they use the drop in speed to attack. From his horse's back, one forces open the door, enters the train and stands guard over the carriage. His Stetson, chaps and denims, and an ornamented gunbelt speak as much as the pearl handled pistols in each hand and the accompanying smell of his unwashed clothes.

He stands, silent, his message clear as his partners also board the train. Two on the roof, their footsteps marking their journey towards the guard's van. Their sure footed movement bespeaks of much experience in train attacks. Several are inside, keeping passengers quiet and making their way to their prize. They wave their guns, pistols, revolvers, around, making it clear that they would have no hesitation in using them. One sends a shot along the length of the carriage, just to make his point. Two men are on either side of the train, their horses keeping pace, ready to receive the gold which is intended to pay the miners at journey's end. Two make their way to the front of the train, ready to dismantle the passenger carriages from the engine and guard. Not to save the passengers, but the shorter the train, the less chance of complications. And, of course, to take control of the engine.

As footsteps thunder above, shots ring out around the carriage and horses gallop alongside, the man opposite me barely flickers an eyelid, as he takes it all in, shuffles the cards and lays out a new game of solitaire on the table.

The train passes Sturry and the law posse, which is waiting for the train to pass takes up the chase. Rifles are aimed and fired; a robber falls from the roof, and the other swings his feet, breaking the window and landing in the carriage. Panic breaks out amongst the robbers as they run up and down the train, getting in each other's way, calling for their horses and firing their guns indiscriminately. The sting of cordite fills the air, mingling with the stench of fear. One robber falls from a stray bullet. Pandemonium rules as uncoordinated shouts, pleas, wails and murmured prayers fill the air. A lawman, star shining in the sun, keeping pace with the train, takes aim from horseback and shoots another bandit cleanly in the head. He also falls, adding to the body count in the centre aisle of the carriage.

The Indians also take advantage of this hiatus. Having taken the chance to board, one brave sneaks behind the man guarding the carriage and silently slits his throat, sending him to the great jailhouse in the sky. Ignoring the broken window glass, he does a quick dance of triumph before the lawman sees him and he

7

jumps through the broken window to land elegantly on his horse and ride away into the Eastcheap desert.

The distant sound of a bugle is heard but the lawmen have no need of the cavalry, the day has been saved. The marshal and his deputies, all now aboard, lug the dead robbers into the next carriage, clear the debris and settle the terrified passengers. They leave the train with a brief salute, a raising of their hats and a swift bow to the ladies.

The train slides quietly into Canterbury West. My cool, elegant companion collects his cards, rises, picks up the dropped pearl handled pistol, places his hat on his head, winks and leaves the train.

His place was taken by a woman in her thirties who shouted into her phone all about her friend's sex life. I put down my book and bowed to the inevitable.

A Day in the Life – 5000 BC

The sun rose, spreading its light across damp grass, sparkling off the dew, sprinkling through the trees, catching a flash of red berry, creeping towards the rocky outcrop and, suddenly, filling the cave with light from a world new born.

The dogs awoke first and the children, then the mothers and the men, hoping to catch a few more minutes. Finally, as the light reached them, the small group of goats tethered at the back of the cave began stirring, bleating, chewing.

Early morning essentials first: water to be fetched, the fire to be built up from the night's banking, the babies to be fed, bed skins to be cleared. While the women did the housekeeping, the men prepared for their day, checking their stock of spears, arrows, discussing the day's tactics. There had been no meat for some days and it was essential to find some today, or they would have to move on, fight other groups for land, build shelters. All of these things took time out from the pleasures of life that this cave afforded. It had plenty of room for all five families; it was easily guarded with a fire and the dogs in the entrance; it had a nearby source of water; and an airflow kept it sweet. They had been living happily here since the beginning of the summer and planned to stay. The women had discovered that grains ground could be made into paste and cooked; a small herd of goats provided milk for the children and, if soured, could be made into a form of cheese. There was an abundance of fruit: the only problem was the meat.

The day began. The young, strong men set out. The older men stayed, knapping the flint for more tools, trying to provide an inexhaustible supply. The young women went out gathering fruit, berries, roots, leaves, grains. Anything they could eat if the men caught nothing. They wondered whether the area was hunted out. The older women watched the children tumbling in the sun with the dogs. Meanwhile, they set to preparing skins for clothing for the coming winter, deftly sewing them together with sinew and needles fashioned from antlers. Others ground yesterday's grains between two heavy stones, and mixed it with water and a little fat saved from the last elk. Someone milked the goats.

The dogs slept, the goats chewed and the babies gurgled. The rhythmic sound of milling and the humming of industry filled the cave. A tune of lazy chatter, with the backbeat of the children's chanting game sounded the passing of time. The sun rose higher, casting a soft shadow into the cave as it rose past the entrance. Cool and sweet, the cave felt like home.

The women returned from foraging, greeted with delight by the children, who were hungry and placated with sweet red berries. Soon, the men could be heard in the distance, cheering and singing: clearly they had met with success. They arrived at the cave, with the children dancing around them, bearing a boar. Better news, too. They had sighted larger prey in the distance and, tomorrow, after a good meal tonight, they would go after it. An aurochs perhaps, or even a mammoth. The evening would be spent planning the morrow's hunt.

The boar was quickly skinned, butchered and hung over the fire in joints. Most of it would be eaten tonight but some parts would be smoked, dried and preserved for emergencies. The fat was collected in hollow receptacles; the bread cooked over hot stones; the roots and leaves baked in the ashes.

Enticed by the heady smell of roasting meat, the soft aroma of baking bread, the sharp tang of herbs and berries, the five families came together, their day's work done, to partake of the feast. The boar's meat was shared out, with the men and the pregnant women feeding first; the bread soaked up the juice from the meat and the roots; the leaves and berries adding flavour and piquancy to the meal. The men, intoxicated from the food and the beer brewed for just such an occasion, sang. Their song became a chant, then a dance as they celebrated the boar, gave thanks for his sacrifice and asked for his guidance in the hunt for the large animal, whatever it was.

The song faded happily, as the twilight darkened and the cave was lit by firelight. The men gave way to the women, singing low, humming the children to sleep. Conversation slowed as preparations for the night took place. The skins were claimed and placed, the fire banked, the dogs quieted.

Then all was still. A mumble, a snore, a whimper and a shuffle. With full bellies, under warm skins, safe, trusted and loved, guarded by the dogs around the fire, the occupants of the cave dreamed of another day just like the one they'd had.

And outside, with the sun on the other side of the world, the moon watched over them with her starry jewels and her cloak of the Milky Way, and she promised them their aurochs.

Crime Story

After the bloody, bitter and prolonged civil war had shuddered into an uneasy peace, the UN decreed that it would be sending in a peace force and therefore the army must be disbanded and all weapons destroyed.

The newly installed president, let's call him President Overlord for now, thought that it was a shame to destroy such beautiful weapons when they could raise much needed cash to replace the money he had spent on the war. Therefore, he contacted an old school friend, who was now a leader of an insurgency group which was in receipt of a generous overseas aid package donated to him by rich and generous Western nations in need of something to salve their ex-colonial consciences. So, with the ready cash, the insurgency leader bought the weapons and used them to bring freedom to, not only his own people, but those around him, whether they wanted it or not.

Now, this leader, shall we say his name is General Landgrab, had also, by way of apparently voluntary donation, become the owner of a rich and fruitful diamond mine. The diamonds were plentiful and of excellent quality, not to say size. They were brought out of the earth by a cheerful workforce who all had wonderful, life-enhancing employment contracts: if they dug out diamonds, they got to keep their lives.

Now, this now successful freedom fighter had occasion to visit a large Western city for an international conference of leaders. He met up with an old colleague in the freedom fighting business, who was now a senior politician half a world away. This man, perhaps called Señor Cocaine, was head of a vast agricultural and pharmaceutical company which was a world leader in certain exports.

One evening, during the conference, these two old friends were enjoying a drink together at the bar, when Señor Cocaine espied a beautiful, elegant and sophisticated woman, and instantly fell in love with her. Her role at the conference was to provide hospitality, and one of her specialities was to provide all delegates with a seemingly unending procession of beautiful girls, none of whom spoke English and all of whom were happy to do anything that the delegates wanted them to. This was because, the harder they worked, the faster they would pay off the substantial loans they had taken out to come to this country, and would be able to start paying the back rent on the room they shared with not more than ten others.

Anyway, to cut a long story short, Señor Cocaine asked Ms Slaver to marry him, and, to his delight, she accepted. To mark their union, Señor Cocaine wanted her to have the biggest and best diamonds in the world, which, of course, he purchased from his friend, General Landgrab. Ms Slaver, now Señora Cocaine, loved the diamonds and wore them often, especially when the media were around.

Now, it just happened that she was not wearing them the day she was kidnapped. Indeed, they formed the basis of the contract, perhaps better known as the ransom. The kidnappers, who wanted the money to finance training in civil unrest and bomb-making, merely wanted the diamonds. They did not want any trouble, so they agreed to return Señora Cocaine unharmed so long as no media, police or public appeal was forthcoming. And so it came to pass.

Now, clearly, our kidnappers, led by Jihad Jim (not his real name, of course), couldn't spend the diamonds, so they took them to another country, one which specialised in diamonds without provenance. They approached Herr Schwarzmarkt, who assured them that he had customers who would be only too pleased to purchase the goods and that no trace of the sale would remain.

Jihad Jim and his colleagues returned to their home city, without the diamonds but with a portfolio of stocks, bonds and shares in carefully selected off-shore companies, and with a guarantee that no nosy bureaucrat would ever be able to help himself to some of it in the name of revenue collection.

That portfolio was stored in a bank vault, in a strong box while Jihad Jim waited to hear from Herr Schwarzmarkt that the diamonds had disappeared without trace. That is, until the bank was raided. Mr. Villain (for it was he) had discovered that the bank vault once was part of a complex series of tunnels, the entrance to which was now sealed with an impenetrable concrete wall. So, while Mr. Villain and two others occupied the front of the bank by collecting all the nice money in the till and the even nicer money in the ATM machines, downstairs, a group of friends blasted the concrete wall away, helped themselves to the bank reserves, and began opening the boxes.

Amongst the insured paste jewels, counterfeit banknotes, guns, stolen art works and Nazi gold, they found the portfolio of stocks, bonds and shares placed there by Jihad Jim and his colleagues for safe keeping. All heavy and three dimensional items disappeared down the tunnel, but the paper was placed in a briefcase and handed to Mr. Villain.

Upon completion of his business at the bank, Mr. Villain left by the front entrance and made his way to the getaway car, a carefully selected stolen black Kashqai, This middle-class family vehicle was the ideal touch of anonymity to allow Mr. Villain to escape. In his desire not to be noticed, and therefore caught, the driver of said getaway vehicle accordingly stopped at the traffic lights.

Passing by were two young men who had just picked up their dole money, had a couple of pints and a few spliffs, and were ready for some fun. Joe dared Mo to open a car door and grab whatever he could. He did so, and found he had a nice briefcase in his hand. With a head full of dope and a body full of adrenalin, he ran as fast as he could for laughing, and bumped into a store detective who was threatening a lad with prosecution.

As Mo and the store detective fell in a heap to the ground, the lad, Jason, couldn't believe his luck. Clutching the litre of vodka to his skinny fourteen-year-old chest, he ran from the shop, only to find himself in the path of a vehicle moving towards the traffic lights from the left.

The driver of the vehicle, Mr. Citizen, executed a perfect emergency stop which allowed Jason to escape into the crowd.

Once past the lights, Mr. Citizen pulled in to the kerbside to pull himself together, stop shaking and take a few deep breaths. As he was doing so, a traffic warden tapped on his window, issued him a parking ticket and a sixty pound on-the-spot fine. Mr. Citizen tried to explain, but the traffic warden was having none of it.

'You see, sir, illegal parking is a crime. And crimes must be punished. Otherwise, what would the world come to?'

By Royal Appointment – a true story

She was a lovely dog. Large, shaggy and black. And easy-going, affectionate and friendly. Well-mannered. But she did have a mind of her own at times. She once got on a bus and sat by the driver waiting for someone to buy her a ticket. If she was told off (which wasn't often), she would take herself to the nearby school kitchen where they would give her biscuits until I responded to their call and collected her. She once slipped her lead and was found lying beneath my usual table in my local.

She also had a very individual way of greeting men whom she thought deserved her special attention. She would place her substantial muzzle between their legs and look up sharply, gazing at them with melting brown eyes. This usually resulted in the chosen man gasping, doubling up and giving me a pleading look for assistance. For myself, this resulted in acute embarrassment.

The first time she did this was to a policeman standing, as policemen do, with legs apart and hips thrust slightly forward. Strangely, no man ever complained: they always laughed it off, their own embarrassment matching mine.

The time I want to tell you about requires some explanation. We lived and worked in a posh girls' boarding school. The dog was welcome and treated as one of the family. I worked in a stand-alone building, the middle floor of which housed form rooms and a small office where the English teachers did their marking.

On this particular evening, I had been working in the office and had taken the dog with me. We left at about 6.45, a little after the last day girls had left for home and the boarders had convened for supper. However, Beatrice York had left her sports bag in her form room and asked her father to get it for her.

Beatrice's father is the Duke of York, a regular face at the school.

However, during this visit, as he was going up the stairs to the middle floor, I was going down the stairs en route to my flat. The dog, at this point, decided to treat him to one of her special greetings. If you can imagine the angle, with the dog being a little higher, it meant that her greeting was all the more effective.

Now, I know that people have varying views on the Duke of York, but you must hand it to him: he is well trained. His skin turned a pale shade of eau de nil, his lips went blue, his eyes flowed and, just for a moment, he ceased breathing. But he did not flinch. He did not wince. He remained standing to attention, looking directly ahead of him as he stretched out his right hand, saying 'Good evening, Miss Cole. I see you have been working late'.

The moral of the story? A cat may look at a king, but it takes a real bitch to get intimate with a duke.

Two Characters in Search of a Hiding Place

It started as a bet and ended as an errand of mercy. My group of mad mates had begun to challenge each other to increasingly bizarre dares, the prize being a free night of as much beer as you can drink. Anyway, my turn had come around and I was challenged to sneak in and spend a whole night in Waterstones. Sneaking in was easy enough. As the manager did his last check, I walked behind him, keeping out of his way behind shelves.

Once alone, though, the thought of a whole night stretching ahead seemed less fun. I checked the café, but everything was locked away. Glad I had brought some sandwiches, I found a comfy chair, took off my shoes, jacket and trousers and settled down for my vigil. Failing to doze, I looked around me and realised that I was in the Drama section.

Thinking that it would be nice to revisit some of my old university texts, I pulled out a *Romeo and Juliet*. I had always liked Juliet but felt that she could have done better than Romeo. Before beginning, I went around to find a couple of other plays, deciding that Chekhov's *The Seagull* would be enough for now. I opened both, to read the first lines and decide which I would read first.

I hadn't really got much beyond 'two hours traffic of our stage' in the Prologue, when I became aware of a presence alongside me. I turned to find a young girl, with a direct, open gaze, old fashioned clothes and a longing look, staring at me.

'Where did you spring from?' I asked.

18

'Please, sir, can you help us?' she replied, with a pleading non-sequitur.

It seemed that she had escaped from somewhere and was hoping not to have to return.

'I am Juliet,' she said. 'Shakespeare had bound me forever with that wimp, Romeo. He talks all the time, never actually gets around to doing anything except the grand dramatic gesture. All those stars, all those jewels in his talk drive me insane. Really, to think I'd kill myself for him! Kill myself to get away more like. He's a self-obsessed, self-pitying, brat. I have got to get away. Please help.'

As you can imagine, I was flummoxed. The question was, how could I help? No, the question was, how did she get out? No, did she really dislike Romeo? I know I thought that about him, but Juliet!

I decided to treat the situation as entirely normal.

'Where do you want to go?'

'Well, as you have opened *The Seagull,* I'd quite like to spend my life with Konstantin. We met, you see, when Chekhov was first writing it. He had checked something in my play and had left it open. So Konstantin and I spent that first night together. I really like him. And he wants to get away from his awful mother, don't you, Sweetheart?'

I realised that there was another person, alongside Juliet. They were quietly holding hands and standing closely.

'Yes,' he said. 'I'm in the same position. My mother is an awful woman, and I only try to kill myself to avoid her. It's got nothing to do with my play. Chekhov just didn't understand.'

19

I wanted to ask how the playwright who invented the characters could fail to understand, but this evening was so odd, that the question seemed superfluous. Instead I asked them what they wanted me to do.

Juliet explained, 'Well. We can only be together if both books are open at the same time in the same room. You would be amazed how rarely that happens. Since 1895, we have had these few stolen moments and just want to disappear to be together. Can you make us disappear?'

I opened one of my cans and took a slug of Fosters while I thought about it. It occurred to me that if they could get out of a book when it was open, they could probably get into a book. So, the question was, which one?

I suggested this to them.

'Yes, said Juliet. That would work. We have thought along those lines ourselves at times. We did think maybe the Grossmiths' *Diary of a Nobody*. The chances of anyone reading that all the way through is fairly minimal. If we hide towards the end, people would be skimming by then and would probably miss us.'

I wasn't so sure: I had quite enjoyed it. I did, however, suggest *The Life and Opinions of Tristram Shandy* not because it is a bad read, but because about two thirds of the way through are some empty pages. These pages are deliberate, part of the humour of the story. If Konstantin and Juliet could somehow get in there and hide in the unprinted pages, they could completely disappear.

They were delighted by this idea and were convinced that it would work. The only problem was, did the shop have a copy? There was nothing on the fiction shelves, on the Classics shelves, on the humour shelves. Eventually, Konstantin found a copy in the reserved pile. It meant that someone would be collecting the book and taking it away from the shop. This would minimise the chance of them being discovered.

I opened the book, read a few pages, then flicked through until I came to the blank section. I put the open book down, closed *Romeo and Juliet* and *The Seagull* and took myself for a walk around the 'mind and spirit' department. When I returned, the book was still there, but I was alone. I sat back in my chair, drank another can, turned off my light and told myself I must have slept.

In the morning, I went to hide before the staff began to arrive, so that I could buy a book. The receipt would prove that I was still there in the morning and I could claim my evening's drunkenness. A stroke of genius hit me, that I should buy the *Tristram Shandy* thereby ensuring their privacy. I shook myself and got a grip, and picked up the latest Terry Pratchett (bless him).

I couldn't resist, though. Turning to the contents page of a complete Shakespeare, I saw, in its traditional place between *Titus Andronicus* and *Timon of Athens* was the play I really didn't expect to see: *The Tragedy of Romeo, Bachelor of Verona.*

I bought the *Tristram Shandy.*

The Little Ships Leave Ramsgate Harbour

'Dad said that you two have known each other for 75 years. Is that right? Would you tell me about how you first became friends?'

Albie looked at his great-grandson, watching him piloting the boat as they joined the formation ready to sail to Dunkirk in commemoration of the evacuation in 1940. He was proud of the boy, but couldn't see how he could really explain about that night.

That night…

Albie was not quite old enough to join up to fight the Nazis, but was looking forward to it. Consequently, when the news came that people were needed to help rescue the BEF from France, the 17 year old didn't hesitate. He climbed aboard the family fishing dingy, Gloria, and set off.

There were ships everywhere, from large naval vessels through the fishermen and lifeboats down to the really little boats, like his. Together they set sail for the coast of France, braving the heavy seas and rising wind. Ahead of them, throughout the sailing, as night came on, they became ever more aware of the flashes of shellfire, the ratatatat of the fighter planes and the calm voice of the navy commander issuing orders through a megaphone.

The larger ships were to anchor off the coast while the smaller ones went in-shore to gather as many men as possible, and to take them back to the larger ships, then go back for more. This was a night when everyone could do their bit for Blighty. If each tiny boat could rescue just one man each, that would be one man fewer left for Hitler.

As ordered, Albie manoeuvred his faithful Gloria towards the sea shore. There were men in the water, alive and dead, men were shouting, gesticulating. Fighters and bombers overhead inflicted as much damage as they could, bullets and shells flew, burst their casings, bursting the heads and bodies of men as they did.

Just off Albie's starboard a body floated, face up, like a star. The lights and flashes flickered across it, making it look alive. Albie started to pull the body into his boat, he felt so desperately sorry for the young man lying dead and abandoned.

'Leave him', someone shouted. 'He's a goner'.

But Albie couldn't do it. He thought that if the rescuers acted so callously, what chance did the Empire have? He didn't know the man was dead, so he ignored the order and pulled him into the boat.

As he did so, the young man coughed, spewed water and croaked, 'I'm Ted. Thank you.'

Ted was breathing, but his lungs were rasping, and he was bleeding profusely from a wound in his left thigh. Ignoring the commands again and instead of taking Ted to the hospital ship, Albie made straight for home. He used his belt as a tourniquet and talked to Ted throughout the journey. After all, he had been told to rescue one man, to not leave him for Hitler. And he had. He had rescued Ted, not even being prepared to leave his body for Hitler.

During that journey, the two young men shared their hopes, their fears. They talked of how they would win the war, what they would do afterwards. Ted told Albie about how he loved working with wood and Albie talked of his passion for fishing. By the time they got back, it was as if they had known each other all their lives. And they knew that they would never be parted.

On their return to Ramsgate Harbour, Ted was taken from Albie and whisked to the emergency hospital set up at Manston. As the ambulance left, Ted shouted, 'Admiral Harvey, 8 o'clock, the day after the war ends.'

And that's where they were, both of them, on the 9th of May, 1945. Ted had lost his leg and so spent the war in a radio hut somewhere in the Midlands. Albie, so it turned out, had had his hearing damaged at Dunkirk, and spent his war in a munitions factory.

They had a pint; they had another. And even now, in their nineties, they meet for a pint at Harvey's.

Albie's great-grandson, now piloting a modern vessel across the Channel on a bright, calm, clear day, looked at the two old men. Both had tears on their cheeks. They were holding hands and they were dreaming of the lives they might have lived if they had been born fifty years later.

The Kindness of Strangers

'That'll be £15.59,' the girl on the checkout said.

Elsie brandished her debit card, waving it around. The girl indicated the machine, and asked Elsie to put the card into it and enter her PIN. Elsie did as she was asked and entered her PIN.

'1559', she said.

The girl frowned. 'You're not supposed to say it out loud,' she admonished.

However, the machine refused the PIN and the girl asked Elsie to try again.

'Oh dear,' Elsie said, 'I might have put the wrong number in. I'll try again.'

But this time, no number came to mind. She asked the girl if she knew, but of course, she didn't. A young mother in the lengthening queue tutted with impatience. A gaggle of schoolgirls sniggered and a toddler started to wail.

The various sounds of disapproval filled Elsie's head, making it ever harder for her to remember her number.

The girl said, 'Could you pay with cash?'

Elsie brightened. She looked into her purse, and found £15.52. She looked again but the other seven pence was just not there.

'I don't suppose…' Elsie said, 'No of course not, it's the machine, isn't it?'

She looked around helplessly, into the blank faces of the schoolgirls, the frowning face of the young mother and the red, angry face of the toddler. The queue seemed to go a long way back.

Someone shouted, 'For God's sake, get a move on. We've got lives, you know.'

Elsie felt the tears prick, the sense of shame rise and the confusion fill her head. She was, by now, incapable of making a decision.

The girl, who seemed patient, said, 'Would you like to leave something? Then you could pay for the rest.'

That seemed sensible, but Elsie needed everything. She thought about changing the bread to a cheaper one, but that would mean going back into the shop. Or maybe she could do without the orange, but Mr. Blair had said that she had to eat 5 a day.

She hesitated. She pondered. She was aware that a tide of frustration and anger was behind her. The girl pressed the button for help and an officious woman arrived, and tried to bully Elsie into just leaving the shop.

At this point, a young man strode forward. His face furious, his fists clenched, his stride determined.

'What is the matter with you all? Can't you all see that this lady needs help? How would you feel if someone treated your mother the way you are treating her?' He pulled a 10 pence piece out of his pocket and flung it on the counter. He packed Elsie's groceries into a carrier bag and guided her to a bench.

'Now, sweetheart, let's sort you out,' he said. 'You've got your shopping. Do you need to do anything else, or do you just want to go home?'

Elsie had had enough. 'I want to go home.'

But the anger in the shop had got into her head. She couldn't, for now, remember where she lived. She thought it was St. Anne's Road, but she couldn't be sure. She tried to explain this to the young man.

'Come on, love. I'll take you to St. Anne's Road and see if you can remember from there.'

But when they reached St. Anne's Road, Elsie's house had somehow been transformed into a modern block of flats. Elsie felt so ashamed. She had put the young man to all that trouble for nothing.

'Do you have a mobile?' he asked, kindly.

She handed him her mobile. He began to scroll through the phone numbers and found one for 'Grey Gables Care Home'. He called it.

'I have a nice lady here who is not quite sure where she lives. Are you missing someone?'

There was an anxious voice on the other end of the call.

He took her to Grey Gables, where she was met by Shirley, her favourite care worker.

'Now, Elsie, where have you been? What is this shopping? You know you don't have to buy groceries, we give you all the food you need.'

She thanked the young man, who asked her out for a drink.

A year later, Shirley married the nice young man, and Elsie was the guest of honour.

The Old Rocker

U3A Open Day was in full swing. Old friends greeted each other, group members chatted, and newcomers looked around anxiously.

An old man shuffled in, incongruously dressed in a leather bomber jacket and drainpipe jeans. He wandered around, clearly looking for something. Bev approached him and, in her usual kindly way, offered to help: he said that he had heard that there was a course on rock'n'roll. Accordingly, Bev showed him where the 'The Old Rockers' sat but suggested that he might like to browse the other tables, too.

He did. He admired the art, nodded to the knitters, shuddered at the Shakespeare and chatted to the nice ladies on the writing table.

He was stooped, with an old fashioned comb-over, clearly dyed black but there was something about him: he stood out from the crowd, but it was hard to see why. His eyes were somehow compelling. There was an attraction, a presence about him that belied his frailty.

He reached the 'Old Rockers' table, behind which sat a man with slicked back hair and a woman in a twinset with just a hint of a net petticoat under her skirt. Decorating the table was a selection of LP covers, showing Chuck Berry, Gene Vincent and others. The couple introduced themselves as Andy and Janet and they explained how they were trying to revive the love of early rock'n'roll and that their group met monthly to appreciate the music. But now they were running a course exploring the origins of rock'n'roll.

They asked the stranger about himself. Was he a big fan? Clearly he was American. Had he ever seen any of the greats?

What did he most love about the music? Everything, he said. It crossed race boundaries, it spoke youth to youth, it was wild, free and unfettered. It celebrated life.

Fascinated by his passion, they questioned him further. They invited him to talk about himself. He thought that when rock'n'roll was young, he was young, he felt that as he grew older, and the music became tamer, both he and it lost something.

His voice quietened, his shoulders slumped, his eyes teared. Sotto voce, he said, 'Really, I, that is, it, died in the casinos in Las Vegas. It became fat, over-decorated, needing to be fed artificially, not able to sustain itself.'

Changing the subject in an attempt to lighten his mood, they asked him how he came to be living in England.

'I left my job in '77, I had a sort of breakdown and I had to get away, to disappear, to be dead. But it's a long time ago now and I think it is time I rejoined the living'.

They could do nothing but ask him if he was interested in joining their course.

Indicating his interest, he asked them where they would be starting. He supposed that they would begin with Bill Haley, the first big rock'n'roll name. Or perhaps they would be looking back before to the beginnings with blues and blue grass.

'No', was the emphatic response. 'We begin with the King. Blue Suede shoes, Jailhouse Rock, Heartbreak Hotel'.

The stranger nodded approval. His ice blue eyes bore compellingly into theirs, twinkling: a half smile lit up his face as the years fell from him. He stood up, taller, straighter, elegant.

The Old Rocker

His bomber jacket and jeans no longer looked incongruous. His charisma caused the room to pause, a silence to fall and everyone to turn to the stranger.

Nodding to Andy and Janet, he moved with an easy swagger towards the door. Andy called out, 'What is your name?'

Turning his head, he growled over his shoulder in a deep Mississippi drawl, 'You know my name,' and left the building.

Then Andy and Janet gaped at each other. Everyone in the hall remained still, looking at the back of the door as it swung shut. After a long pause, Janet put everyone's thoughts into words. 'Elvis Presley is alive and well and a member of the Thanet U3A'.

You Shall Go to the Ball

Cinderella had spent all day preparing her step-mother and step-sisters for the ball. She had fed them, bathed them, made their gowns, dressed them, decorated them and seen them leave. She sat quietly by the hearth in the kitchen with a hot cup of tea and wriggled her toes in the warmth as she welcomed the quiet.

Suddenly, with great commotion, and in a shower of gold sparks, a magical woman appeared in the kitchen.

'I am your fairy godmother,' she exclaimed. 'I have come to ensure that you, too, will go to the ball. You will have a gown grander than all the rest, a carriage with horses and footmen to arouse astonishment, and shoes that will be made of crystal.'

Cinderella looked calmly at the woman, and down to her feet, free of all shoes, resting at last.

'No, I don't think so,' she said. 'Thanks and all that, but I really think I just want to sit here.'

'But just think,' the godmother exclaimed, 'you will meet the Prince. You will dance with fine gentlemen and see all the wonderful gowns. And just think of the food!'

'It's really nice of you,' Cinderella countered, 'but I've had enough of fine gowns and rich food for today. What you could do for me that would be really handy, is to give me some kind of tool for peeling vegetables. Oh, and a really comfy pair of slippers.'

Exasperated, the fairy godmother waved her wand and on the table appeared a small gadget with a small blade. And next to the chair was a pair of sheepskin moccasins

.

'You don't know what you're missing, you silly girl. And, by the way, these things will only last till midnight.' And with that, she disappeared, never to be seen again.

But Cinderella was cleverer than the fairy godmother gave her credit for. She spent the evening copying the slippers in the best scraps she could find and made detailed drawings of the gadget.

Having had a lovely, relaxing evening, she was ready when her step-mother and step-sisters got home, full of the ball, the gowns, the gentlemen, the food. They were most of all excited by the behaviour of the prince who had not, as expected, chosen a bride. Instead, he had wandered about, staring at everyone's feet, as if looking for someone in particular.

The next morning, having cooked and cleaned up from breakfast, Cinderella went off to market as usual. However, before doing the chores, she popped into the patents office and dropped in the drawings of the vegetable peeler. She also went into a shoemaker's shop to sell the pattern for the moccasin.

Cinderella never married the prince, never even met him. Instead she married the shoe-maker, who found a way to mass produce the slippers. They made enough money from her peeler and slippers to buy a nice cottage in which to raise her large, healthy and bouncy family.

Many years later, as she sat by her fireside, in a big, comfy chair, with a hot, fresh cup of tea and the latest great-grandchild murmuring happily in his cradle, she smiled at her loving husband, and as she wriggled her toes, she thought of that night long past and wondered how her life might have turned out if she had, after all, gone to the ball.

The prince never married, but amassed a huge collection of women's shoes.

The Dark Time

'Ok gentlemen, shall we get started? There are seven of us present, there have been a few apologies which I'll deal with later, and a message that I couldn't fully make out but I think it says someone will be late. Is everyone happy with the minutes from last year? Ok. So, on with the first item. Dates.'
'

The seven holiday reps shuffled. This was always the boring part. Most of them were happy with the same date each year, but some always wanted to argue.

A beautiful young man with a quiver, a bow, an elaborate gold headdress and blue skin spoke first. 'I'd like to go for November the eleventh to the fifteenth, if that's ok. I think it makes my Diwali first.'

'Of course it doesn't, Rama,' said the skeleton wearing a scream mask. 'I'm always first because I have the last day of October. There's no problem with that, is there?

'So long as I can come next on the fifth of November,' said the gentleman in the scorched seventeenth century clothes and goatee.

'That's settled then,' said the Chairman. 'So, November's done. What about December?'

A thin man in a stovepipe hat and a suit made of stars and stripes interrupted. 'No, Thanksgiving is always in November. This year I'd like the 26th. I don't think that interferes with anyone.'

The man in bright blue with spiky blond hair spluttered. 'You always say that, and let's face it, you shouldn't really be here. We are all representations of dark time holidays, brightening the long nights with lights and parties. I'm not even sure about Halloween, or you, Guy, come to think of it.'

'My fireworks are the highlight of the festival of lights, with the bonfires, we give light and heat in those dark, damp November evenings. And I'm about celebrating democracy. It's hard enough with Halloween muscling in on my act, without you casting aspersions, Jack Frost.'

'Oh, so you don't think honouring the dead and playing games with apples and lighting all those yummy smelling pumpkins are important, huh?'

'Gentlemen, gentlemen, please. I represent Hanukkah, and this year we would like December the sixth to the fourteenth. But really, do we need all this name calling every year? Aren't we all about celebrating being human, and honouring the dark of the year by lighting it up, whether it be with pumpkins, fireworks or menorahs. I'm sure even Thanksgiving has a purpose.'

'Absolutely. I represent freedom and new beginnings. I lead people to consider their blessings. And to do that at the time when the light fails reminds everyone that the light will return.'

'That's my job,' said Jack Frost, on the winter solstice – December twenty-first as usual please – but I don't mind you sharing, Thanksgiving, especially as some of us are sort of geography specific.'

Things seemed to calm down, and to lighten the atmosphere, Rama asked the Chairman, 'Would you like a different date this year, or will the twenty-fifth of December do, as usual?'

But the good natured ripple of laughter was abruptly interrupted. The door flew open, and a sudden gust of wind blew in till receipts, tatty wrapping paper, plastic bags, crumpled tinsel and a large man, in an expensive suit, smoking a huge cigar.

'Ah, I'm glad you're all here. Let me introduce myself. I am Profit Moneybags Consumer Capitalism. My company has bought up the last quarter of the year. And you are all redundant. Please leave the building as soon as a security officer arrives to accompany you to the door.'

The Chairman drew himself up to his full height, drew his red coat around him, smoothed his bushy white beard and challenged. 'Mr. Consumer Capitalism, We have been lending celebration to these months for time immemorial. Well, for several hundreds of years at least for some of us. Between us we represent light, warmth, continuity, renewal, endings, beginnings, democracy, gratitude and giving. We help the humans through the cold, the dark and the damp. We bind them together through fun, laughter, giving, sharing, ritual and custom. Do you really think that your cold, calculating approach to the Dark Time can wipe out all of that?'

'I saw off the Greek and Roman gods. I saw off the Norse gods and I will see the end of you!' he thundered. My company is simply going to do away with all these fiddly celebrations. We are going to begin on the first of September by flooding all the shops with dressing up clothes, fireworks, cards, masks, sweets, tinsel baubles, plastic trees, plastic toys and put them all in plastic bags. That way, the money will keep rolling in without any gaps and no-one will have to remember which date is which festival. Look in the shops now. In some of them you will even find Easter eggs. And when we have fully established Winterval, we will open the shops for all time, with year-round sales and advertising. And no-one will know the dark days because the lights will never go off.

And for a while, it seemed as if he was right.

The seven were escorted from the building and they took themselves into a nearby public house. Several beers later (and stronger stuff for some), they started to remember how strongly their constituents had felt.

'Well,' said Thanksgiving, 'three hundred and eighteen million Americans celebrate me every year, and they don't seem to care that I am close to Christmas. In fact, many of them see me as the beginning of the holiday season. And you, Rama, your seven hundred and fifty million followers love Diwali. And Hanukkah is celebrated all over the world and has been for thousands of years.'

'Every time there is an election, you get remembered, Guy Fawkes. And your fireworks now celebrate everything from birthday parties to the new year.'

'And when the solstice comes round, the light starts to return and there is nothing that anyone can do about that,' rejoined Jack Frost.

'And practically every child under twelve loves trick or treating,' added Halloween and let's face it, the whole world does Christmas, whatever religion it is. For Christians, of course, it is holy, but even for non-Christians it is a time of togetherness and giving.'

'Right lads,' decided the Chairman. 'Let's get back in there and give that moneybags what for.'

And they did. Rama shot him with the arrows, and set off fireworks. Jack Frost froze him, and then went sledging. Guy Fawkes set him on fire, and ate a toffee apple while he watched. Halloween threw eggs at him and made him hand over all his sweeties. Thanksgiving cooked the pumpkin lamps into pie and wouldn't give him any. And Hanukkah and Christmas bundled him into a giant sack, put him on a sleigh and sent him away forever.

'Ok,' said the Chairman. 'Back to the meeting. Item number two. What are we going to do about too much eating?'

Lost in LAX – Another True Story

I had enjoyed three and a half wonderful weeks travelling across the United States from New York to Los Angeles on a coach tour and was now about to fly to San Francisco for an extension of that tour. Eight of us from the tour were going on to San Francisco, and we arrived at the airport together, expecting to go through the formalities as a group. However, when I tried the self-check-in machines, I had a message telling me to check in at the desk. I told the rest to go on without me, that I would join them 'airside'.

I joined the very long queue for check-in and was standing in line patiently (I try always to be patient in airports, impatience only leads to frustration, anger and impotence) when an official asked to see my ticket. On seeing it, she directed me to the self-check-in machines. I explained that I had had that message and she told me to go to a ticket purchase desk where the queue was much shorter.

A short while later, a very elegant and sweet lady informed me that I had no ticket. I tried to explain, but she said that the company clearly had printed my ticket before it was confirmed with the airline. I had no ticket. She told me to phone my company and I did so – on a small mobile in the middle of a major airport, with all the noise and bustle around me. I was panicking, angry and frightened. I got through to the emergency number, which turned out to be someone in San Francisco who told me that I would have to contact the main company in London.

At this, I lost it. I panicked, I cried, I shouted. I told him that it was the middle of the night in London and Sunday night at that. He told me to phone him back in fifteen minutes.

Those fifteen minutes were a very long fifteen minutes. During the next call (and the one after, and the one after that), I was repeatedly told to call back. Apparently, he was not able to call me. I sat on the floor and wept. Not only did I not have a ticket, an idiot on the phone, but also the time allowed for check in was passing much more quickly than the phone call time was going.

Then my mind kicked in. Plan B. If I don't make this flight, I will simply buy another flight to San Francisco on my credit card, reasoning that there must be one every couple of minutes, get a taxi to my hotel from the airport (I would have missed my transfer) and charge the company for the expenses, for negligence and for emotional trauma. This is America, after all.

Once I had a Plan B, I was fine. I'm always the same. I panic, then cry, then Plan B happens and everything is possible. I can cope with anything. The next time I called, he said that the ticket was sorted and I could check in at the purchase desk, as it was a new purchase. As luck would have it, it was the same nice lady.

The ticket had come through. However some authorisation had not. By this time I didn't care. It was past the check in time anyway and Plan B was beginning to look better and better. I could even take time to get a drink to calm things down.

While she was explaining things to me, the authorisation came through. She accepted my check in, saying that once I was in, they would hold the plane for a few minutes. I had go to the elevator to the right and go up one floor to Security, but I would have to hurry.

The situation was more complex now: I had checked in and my luggage had gone. The gate had an impossibly large number on it, suggesting that there were several miles to walk. The plane was due to take off in less than ten minutes. Plan B was still possible but would be harder to implement.

I hurried. The lift took forever. Then… it went down.

The lift door opened and there was a young Hispanic man, all smiles and brass buttoned uniform, with a very elderly, very frail couple. They all got into the lift. The young man was so nice, that I blurted out the whole story to him.

He asked me to give him my boarding card, and when we reached Security, he helped the elderly couple out of the lift and told us all to stay exactly where we were. There was little else I could do: he had my boarding pass and Security was teeming with what looked like hundreds of people. The old gentleman took his belt and shoes off in preparation for security. A minute or so later, my young man returned with an electric passenger cart. He told me to get on, bodily lifted the couple onto the back, ignoring the state of undress of the man, and drove directly into the crowd until we reached the Security desk whereupon he waved the boarding passes at the officials and threw our hand luggage onto the conveyor belt ahead of everyone else's.

Then he yelled at the couple to hold on tight and he drove. We went at full speed, down endless corridors, careering around corners, weaving between people, with him shouting to get out of the way, and blasting his siren. The cart swerved and skidded, slowed and speeded, turned and raced. The poor, shocked couple on the back were holding on for dear life, the man still clutching his belt.

Eventually, we screeched to a stop at the gate: he slammed my boarding pass on the counter and said, 'She's here!' Without turning a hair, the girl on the desk told me to board immediately.

Then the walk of shame through the plane: I was easily recognised as the one who had held up the flight, and of course, my seat was right at the back as I was the last to check in. And just to make the occasion even more surreal, half-way down I heard, 'I should have known it was you!' My travel companions? No. A colleague from work who just happened to be on the same flight.

One more moment of surreality. As I had jumped off the cart at the gate, ready to hand my nice young man an extravagant tip, I noticed his name badge – Jesus. So that is how I was saved by Jesus, smiling in a lift, at Los Angeles International Airport.

The Vegetable Plot

Sally always won all the prizes on the vegetable stall in the church fete. Her carrots were long, sweet and perfectly shaped, her onions beautifully globular and her lettuces crisp, green and shining.

But this year, she outdid herself. Everything was bigger, brighter, more tasty and juicier than ever. Felicity was desperate to know her secret. It was no good asking her, because she said she didn't have any secret. So, the ladies of the knitting circle decided to invite Sally to join them.

'You must be lonely since Bill went,' said Felicity in the first meeting. 'I'm surprised you didn't go with him.'

'Well,' explained Sally, 'He works all the time now he's in America and even though the boys are in boarding school, I don't want them to think that both of their parents are inaccessible.'

'I suppose it gives you a lot more time for your garden,' furthered Felicity. 'Clearly something is different this year. What have you done that is different?'

'Well,' suggested Sally, 'I have put a lot more fertiliser on this year. I suppose that must have helped. But the patch is very fertile anyway. I'm sure I don't do anything special. I just have green fingers, I suppose.'

Felicity and Marjorie exchanged furtive glances. Later, making the tea in the kitchen, Marjorie said, 'Fertiliser, hm? I wonder what sort exactly?'

Felicity said, 'And already fertile. Remember that 'uncle' who suddenly died a couple of years ago when he was staying with them? Let's push her on the fertiliser.'

So, over a cup of tea, Marjorie asked, 'What fertiliser exactly, Sally?'

'Nothing you can't get in the garden centre,' replied Sally, 'dried bone, dried blood, potash for minerals. You know, organic stuff.'

That was enough to convince Felicity and Marjorie that heinous deeds had been perpetrated. They met the next day at dusk to have a look in Sally's garden. They had taken the precaution of getting her out of the way by persuading Lily to invite her to dinner on the pretext that Lily had been let down by a dinner guest and couldn't have thirteen at table.

Climbing awkwardly over the back wall, they ventured into the garden. The vegetable plot was near the back wall but between the vegetables and the compost heap was a hole, a large, deep, gaping hole. Clearly this was due to be an extension of the vegetable plot. A man, scruffy, probably homeless, looked over the wall and asked if they could spare any change. Looking at him, and looking at the hole, Marjorie shouted, 'Go, leave. Don't ever come back to this village if you fear for your life.' Alarmed, and not a little disconcerted, he left rapidly. Shaken, the two ladies also left rapidly.

The following Sunday, Sally invited them to tea. And of course they accepted, on condition that she showed them around the garden. The vegetable plot was glorious, the shrubbery was dense, the beds blooming and the fruit trees bursting. There was no sign of the hole except for a well tilled area of clean earth. The two exchanged meaningful glances.

Later, over tea, they were hesitant to share the beetroot sandwiches, such purple blood-red beetroot that is rarely seen. But Felicity forced herself, not wanting to arouse suspicion in Sally that they were on to her.

'If you're not hungry, Marjorie, I could give you some beetroot to take with you. It's a new strain, only just developed. It has a lovely flavour, very sweet, but with a touch of iron behind it.'

This was an excellent idea. Because Marjorie's husband, Peter, a chemistry teacher in the local secondary school, shared Marjorie's suspicions, mostly of course because of the way she had explained them to him. He was to take the beetroot to the laboratory and check its chemical make-up. He was instructed particularly to look for anything that could be human traces. He explained that his laboratory was not set up for such detailed analysis but he could probably find something that could help.

And he did. He found blood, bone and potash, just as Sally had said. Then he came to his senses and told them to stop being so ridiculous.

However, Felicity and Marjorie faced Sally with what they still believed to be the truth. Of course, she laughed at them, just like Peter had. 'I told you I used blood, bone and potash. I also use my own compost. Of course there will be organic traces. And don't forget that is where we put the dog. Oh, for heaven's sake, ladies, get a grip.'

Shamefacedly, they apologised and said that they wanted to make amends.

'I'm not sure that is necessary,' said Sally, 'but to let bygones be bygones, why don't you and your husbands come to dinner and I will cook you a meal made up out of the vegetables from my garden. That way I will know that you trust me.' Narrowing her eyes and dropping her voice, she told them, 'If not, I will tell the whole village and the police what you have done. I'm not sure if slander is a crime but I will find out. Come to dinner and all will be forgotten and forgiven. I won't even mention it to Bill when he gets back.'

So, on Saturday night, Felicity and George, Marjorie and Peter the Chemistry teacher gathered at Sally's house for a sumptuous meal of creamed mixed mushroom soup, stuffed peppers, onions and beefsteak tomatoes, and a delightful summer pudding. Replete, they all laughed at their stupidity and apologised profusely. Sally openly forgave them and toasted a future full of friendship and trust. The wine flowed, then the cognac and eventually they all dropped off to sleep.

The village was devastated to hear that Marjorie, Felicity and their husbands had all been killed on their holiday abroad. The following year, Sally won all the prizes at the County Show and has been invited to take part in a television series about expert amateur gardeners.

The Locksmith's Revenge

Joan had been working at the bakery since she left school. She was happy there, with the Farriners. She lived with them in the flat above the shop and they treated her like the daughter they had never had. For Joan, they were the parents she had lost. Her job was to prepare and kneed the dough, fetch the fuel in from outside and keep the oven hot. Mr. Farriner shaped and baked the bread and pastries, and Mrs Farriner kept the shop. They had always been fun, and often, during quiet times they would play around in the back room.

Recently, Joan had met a nice young man, Will. They went out together, often across the river to the theatre. Sometimes to an ale house, or just walked the beloved streets of London Town, arm in arm. The Farriners thought the world of him.

Will was apprenticed to a locksmith and was nearing the end of his training. He was trying to persuade Joan to join him when he set out on his journeyman years, he as a jobbing locksmith and she as a jobbing baker. Even though he was offering marriage on any terms she wanted, she still hesitated. She wasn't sure she wanted to leave London and the safety of the Farriners. She definitely wanted to marry Will, but wanted to be able to stay close to what was her whole world. She just wasn't brave enough to start out on the life Will was offering. Despite all of his persuasion, she would not budge.

Even though Will was not the jealous type, he did feel that Mr. Farriner had a hold over Joan that seemed to go beyond employer and landlord, but no matter how much Joan explained how much she owed to the Farriners, Will still felt their influence was too strong.

Will decided, after much thought, that he would give Joan an ultimatum. Either she married him straight away and agreed to accompany him or he would find another woman. Deep in his heart though, he knew she would not agree, and he also knew that he would back down, for he loved Joan beyond all else. He was beginning to realise that she would not leave London, and that he would have to choose between Joan and a career. He denied it to himself but he sort of knew that he would choose Joan and a life as an employee, that he would never be a master locksmith. If only Joan could see that she was denying her future children a life of comfort and plenty.

Anyway, he set out to present her with the ultimatum, feeling that it might be enough to change her mind. He bought a pretty posy of flowers and a sweet ring, engraved with their initials. However, when he reached the bakery, he could see, through the door in the back room, Mr. Farriner and Joan were dancing. They were jumping around, and they had their arms around each other. Joan was laughing and showing her lovely throat to him, and when he stopped singing, she reached up and kissed him.

Unknown to Will, Mr Farriner and Joan had played this game, for game it was, since Joan was a newcomer to the bakery. There was nothing in it but fondness, and Mrs Farriner was sitting in the room, out of Will's sight. Will, however, felt that his earlier suspicions, denied by Joan, were vindicated. He turned on his heel, left the bakery and decided to find some way to punish Mr. Farriner and Joan.

It was early September so Will had to wait until late for dark, and for the warm streets to quieten. Some time after midnight he made his way through the now black streets towards Pudding Lane. The roads were slick with dried matter, it not having rained for some weeks; the overhanging upper storeys prevented any light from the moon reaching the street; all householders were in bed so it was quiet, dark, peaceful.

Approaching Farriner's bakery, Will felt himself angry, vengeful. He easily unlocked the door and let himself in. He had no real idea of what he was going to do, but thought perhaps he would put too much salt in the night's bread, or break some of the equipment. He wanted revenge for his plans going awry. Going into the back room, he saw that one of the ovens was still alight, presumably so that it would be hot ready for the morning. An idea came to him. He opened the oven door and stirred up the flames with the bellows. Then he left, intending to call the fire fighters to a danger in Pudding Lane. Farriner would be fined, and possibly closed down. That will teach them!

However, the plan did not quite work. Will couldn't find his way to the fire fighter's house in the dark, and decided instead to mention it in the morning. But, in the bakery, one of the stirred up coals fell out of the oven and onto the matting below. In the dry, hot atmosphere of a summer night, the coal set the matting alight. Mr. Farriner awoke with the sounds of crackling from below. He woke his wife and Joan so that all three could climb out of the window, across the narrow gap into the house opposite.

Joan was afraid of heights and chose instead to wait for help.

As Will made his way back towards the river, he became aware of a bright orange glow behind him, realising that the oven had caused a fire. Starting in the Farriner's kitchen, the fire rose easily through the seven storeys of the Farriner's dwelling, leapt without hesitation across the divide to the next house, then from building to building, along street after street through the warren of wooden dwellings. People swarmed in terror towards the river, but buckets of water had no effect. Will tried to get the right people to act but there was an apparent disbelief until it was too late.

In all, about seventy thousand homes were lost, eighty-seven churches, including the great church of St. Paul, and thousands of uncounted poor.

Later, living in guilty penury in a French monastery, Will heard that the first victim of the fire was a serving maid at Farriner's bakery in Pudding Lane where the fire was thought to have begun. The Farriners themselves survived the fire and always insisted that the bakery had been left completely safe.

A Modern Christmas Carol

'And so, as Tiny Tim observed, God bless Us Every One!' read Tom, as he closed the book. 'My dad used to read this to me every Christmas Eve. Well, my lad, it's time to get you back to your mother's.'

An hour later, Tom was on Stella's doorstep, dropping off their son.

Stella said, for the umpteenth time, 'Why don't you come here for Christmas? Nick would love it, and it would be nice for you to have some company.'

But Tom refused, once again allowing his pride to lead his decisions. He had left Stella and Nick when there had been one too many fallings out over his writer's ambitions. A successful writer of thrillers, Tom yearned to write more literary fiction but Stella simply didn't understand his need. So he had moved to his own flat where he could write in peace. They shared custody of Nick and still got along well, but Tom couldn't bear her patronising attitude to his ambitions.

He wished them both a happy Christmas and went back to his flat. He had planned to spend the Christmas season working on the novel he had at last begun. He would be uninterrupted and able to concentrate.

However, no sooner had he returned and fired up the laptop but his sister phoned. She had had a few drinks with friends and was in full nostalgia mode.

'Remember that night we woke up to open our stockings before mum and dad had gone to bed? And that Christmas mum got pissed on home-made wine and we had to do dinner? What about the Christmas...' and she went on and on.

Tom also remembered the Christmas mum had been in hospital, and the first after dad died, and the Christmas he had spent alone when Stella had to work. He listened to his sister going on and hummed politely.

Eventually she rang off and Tom got back to the computer. But the phone sounded again. 'Hey Tom, I heard you were going to be on your own,' boomed Joey, his oldest friend. Come to ours, there'll be loads of us there. Tom explained about his writing and his desire for solitude. But he was interrupted by a text from a newer mate, inviting him to what sounded like a drunken binge for singles. 'But I'm not single,' he thought, with a pang.

But at this point, he no longer wanted to write, and decided to treat himself to a scotch. As he sat with his drink, looking into the flames of his gas fire, he thought about how he would spend the holiday. But he also thought about Stella saying that she was thinking about going to New Zealand. Suddenly, Tom realised that his selfish needs had driven her away and that she was taking Nick with her. He would never see either of them again.

The combination of the scotch and the fear of loss caused a pain in his chest. The pain worsened as he struggled for breath. He thought that he would die alone on Christmas Eve and no-one would find him until after the holidays; he had chased everyone away in his arrogance. Struggling to calm himself, he forced himself to breathe slowly and deeply as he reached for the phone. But as he dialled 999, the pain eased and he realised that he had suffered a panic attack.

So, instead of dialling 999, he called Stella to ask more about New Zealand. He really thought that if they went, he might as well be dead.

'Yes,' Stella said. 'I am thinking of going. There are some really good tours, and I might try to take in Australia while I'm there. The only problem is that it is difficult in our summer and I don't really want to take Nick out of school. I'll probably leave it for now.'

'It's a holiday you're talking about,' stammered Tom. 'I thought... I thought...' and he began to cry.

'For god's sake, Tom. Call yourself a taxi and get yourself over here. Do it now. I have had enough of this nonsense. You are clearly incapable of looking after yourself. You can write whatever the hell you like, but I am not prepared to worry any more. And while you're at it, call Joey and your sister. They've been on at me and they think you are depressed or suicidal. I think you're an idiot.'

Tom got into a taxi, called and reassured his friend and sister on the way, and found his way back into the arms of his family. He held Stella and Nick in his arms, and buried his face in Stella's hair. Home at last. And to stay.

And so, as tactile Tom observed, God bless Us Every One!

Three Characters, a Thousand Words and a Plot

Sue had to write a story, and she had no idea what to write. For nearly two months she ran scenarios through her head but nothing took root and nothing developed into a story. In the end she sat at her computer, with her hands on the keyboard and went into stream of consciousness.

Three characters: that would be right. Ok, a young woman. Let's call her Jean, no, Linda.

'Oh, please, if you haven't got a story, you could at least give me a nice name. What about Violetta?'

Sue thought about it. Violetta sounded nice.

'If I'm Violetta, I would be dark haired, with flashing eyes, of Southern European stock. You know, passionate. I'd be perfect for a spy thriller. You could put me up against a beautiful blonde Scandinavian type man who is a spy and needs to be taken down.'

'If I'm to be a beautiful, blonde, Scandinavian type, then I don't want to be in a spy thriller. My name is Thor and I want to be in a fantasy piece about gods. I could be the god of thunder and Violetta could be the goddess of passion.'

'Don't be so silly. This isn't a story for kids. Gods and all that stuff. Leave that to Marvel films. I want to be in a full-blooded spy thriller. And you are not Thor. That's such a silly name. You are Anders, from Finland, on the Russian border.

Sue intervened. She reminded them that it was her story, and she would decide the names, the genre and the relationships. An older gentleman coughed politely.

'Excuse me, I am Jonathon. A calm, reliable, well-mannered, older but still handsome Englishman who is married to Violetta and I resent this young man moving into my story. I understand that Violetta is a passionate young woman, but she is no spy. This story is surely one of a love triangle. I am desperately trying to hang on to my marriage while this young man is offering fantasy to lure her away.'

'Darling, I have no interest in this young man. You are all the man I need.'

'You know that is not true. I have turned a blind eye to your extra-marital hobbies just so long as you don't bring them into our story. I appreciate that your need for excitement has led you into spy thrillers, and crime thrillers, and even your occasional dabble with science fiction, but I draw the line at god fantasy.'

'I told him I wasn't interested either, sweetheart. But just like men, neither of you are listening. I just think a nice cosy spy thriller with all three of us would be ideal. You are the Le Carré style English spy, I am the passionate sex-lure and he is the stupid Russian who falls into my trap and gets caught by the super-cool Englishman. You know, James Bond.'

'Firstly, James Bond is not Le Carré, but we'll let that pass. I still think that we naturally fall into a love triangle. I am the faithful and loving but dull Englishman, you are the Italian who has huge emotional needs and seeks to satisfy them with beautiful and handsome young men. They are inevitably stupid and fall for you, never realising that you will not leave me.'

'Listen to the two of you,' chimed in Anders. 'I am not stupid. Yes, I am Scandinavian. I rather like the idea of Swedish. Yes, I am big, blond, handsome, heroic, mysterious yet somehow emotionally vulnerable. But I am not stupid. And I still think that a god fantasy is best. We could set it somewhere like Mount Olympus that is also Asgard. There would be a battle between the brave, noble, fighting spirit of the Norse and the sybaritic and self-indulgent style of the Southern pantheon. It would make a brilliant film. Jonathon, you wouldn't be in this story but I'm sure you can entertain yourself elsewhere for a bit.'

'No,' shouted Violetta. 'Jonathon is my husband, and I will not be in any story that he is not in. And I am not sybaritic and self-indulgent.'

'Well, you are a bit,' said Jonathon.

Enough, thought Sue, this is getting ridiculous. Ok, I have three characters, but still no story. A spy thriller is too complex for a short story, and a god fantasy is, like Violetta said, for kids. And it seems as if Jonathon and Violetta have enough trouble with love triangles without me adding to it. So what's left? A murder? Could Violetta murder Jonathon and Anders is the policeman who solves the puzzle, falls in love with the murderess and protects her from the law?

'Absolutely not! I am not dying so he can be a hero in law and love.'

'And I'm not going to murder you.'

'I quite like that idea. We could sell it to the telly. There's lots of Scandi-crime stuff on. We could split the proceeds.'

Sue stepped in. It's my story, she told them. Any profit from film or telly is mine. Behave!

'I've got an idea,' said Jonathon. We could do a love triangle and do it the other way round. Anders and I fall in love and get together to kill Violetta.'

A chorus of disapproval from both Violetta who did not want to die and Anders who did not fancy Jonathon. And, incidentally, from Sue who was going off the whole idea of this story. Then she had her own idea. At last. There is a light plane crash. Anders is the pilot, and he brings the plane down in a remote area. Both passengers, a married couple, are saved but the woman is injured. The story is about how the two men brave geography, animals and weather to get her to safety.

'I like that. I get to be a loving, trustworthy action hero,' agreed both Anders and Jonathon. We can work together on that.

'I like it too,' said Violetta. I get to be a strong yet vulnerable heroine. Let's go with that story.

Sorry, thought Sue, I've only got a thousand words and they are all used up.

Conflict

He'd always been trouble. The runt of the litter, the one who caused the squabbling. But this time it was different. He'd bit the biggest one, hard, and he knew that the whole lot of them would be after him. So he ran.

He ran between the buildings, through high, narrow alleyways, always looking back, listening and sniffing the air for trouble. Eventually he realised he was lost and would have a hard time retracing his steps. So he crawled into a hole broken through a wall and hid in a dark corner.

It was then that his ever-keen ears picked up a distant whining, becoming a drone and a roar. And then the bombs hit. Crashes of explosions, crashes of buildings falling, the roar of plane engines and the roar of fire. The sharp chemical smell of sudden death. But, hidden in his cave, he felt safe. That is, until an inrush of air caught him and flung him into the wall, and darkness descended.

He awoke some time later, into a new world. Fairly sure that his whole family was dead, he realised that he would have to fend for himself. Thirsty, head aching, every muscle protesting, he pushed his head out of the hole in the wall. And peering in was the biggest cat he had ever seen. A huge, grey, mottled animal, also hungry and apparently waiting for him to appear. He retreated. Something caught the cat's ear and off it went, allowing him to take stock of his surroundings.

The sky was clear and blue but with a pall of yellow smoke blotting out the warmth. The alleyway was nothing but a heap of rubble. And it was ominously quiet. He could hear distant sounds of humans digging and calling; of dogs barking for help, for each other. He tried calling for help but his little voice could not carry through the devastation. The acrid air was all but unbreathable, any water would be evaporated or adulterated. As for food, the rats scurrying through the demolished city indicated that there was none.

With no-one else to pity him, he curled up in his hole, and prepared to die. He remembered the quarrel earlier; his mother growling curses as he fled his brother. In his last moments of lucidity, he realised that he had brought this calamity on his world, and allowed the grief to take him.

Then there was a dog. A large, shaggy animal of the kind he had heard described as a German Shepherd. Huge fearsome teeth, foul doggy breath and a will of iron. The shepherd stuck his head through the hole, sniffing him all over, judging whether or not he was worth the effort. He tried to tell the big dog that he was not worth it, to leave him alone, but the dog was not listening.

There was a shout, a call and the shepherd growled and barked. Another call and he felt the big dog grab him by the scruff of his neck and drag him out of his shelter. He was dumped unceremoniously on the broken paving as the shepherd stood over him, barking with triumph.

More afraid than upset now, he hid his head in his curled up body and attempted to shut out the horrible world.

Then, without warning, searching hands felt him all over. Strong arms picked him up and he felt himself being carried over the rubble and placed gently on a soft surface. The sounds were muffled, voices low, the scent of the place stung with antiseptic.

'He is so young,' said a voice. 'Do you think he can pull through?' The voice spoke in English. He understood a few words, usually of command or scolding, but this voice was different. He was given a strange drink that tasted both sweet and salty, and a piece of bread to eat. As he chewed, he tried to make contact.

'I am Ali, I am seven. I am bad boy,' he stammered.

'Well, Ali, whatever it is you've done, I'm sure you've been punished. I am Claire and I am with Doctors Without Borders and this is James who works for Unicef. I don't expect you understand this, but from now on, my love, you are safe. I can't say the same for Aleppo, I think it's a gonner.

In the Bleak Midwinter

It really was cold. As she struggled down the muddy footpath, her feet slipped in the brown mush left from yesterday's snow. The traffic kicked up so much dirt, mud and grime that it made the hem of her new dress probably unsalvageable. She cursed her brother who had chosen to live in such a place, who needed her to fuss around him just because he was like that. Rounding the corner, the wind blew so sharply and so icily that she was, for a moment, unable to breathe. Birchington in winter is not somewhere anyone with any sense would wish to be!

Shivering, her face stinging and her ankles feeling fragile, she reached the station, only to realise that she had missed the train by a couple of minutes. Minutes that she would have saved, had it not been for the weather. There was no heating in the waiting room, where she would, of necessity, spend the next two hours. Not only was there no heating, but the building was so draughty that it might as well be open to the elements.

Muttering under her breath, she examined her clothing. The lovely new dress was ruined. The new stripy fabric and the latest style. Although the bustle could be a nuisance, there were no hoops. She had always hated the hoops, because one could not see one's feet. Trying to walk in this weather in hoops would have been treacherous. Her warm woollen coat and bonnet had proven unable to cope with such an afternoon. And she was hungry. Even though her brother had provided some refreshment, it was not enough to sustain through this weather.

Realising that she also had no book to read - she had left it with her brother - she took out a notebook, hoping that some sort of inspiration would help pass this time.

Just as she had accustomed herself to the wait, the station manager entered.

'Oh, miss,' he said, 'I didn't realise you were here. Did you know that you have just missed a train? Would you like a nice, warm cup of tea? And maybe a slice of cake? I'll light the fire first.'

And he did, and he brought the tea and cake. And he sent his boy for company. The boy was a cheery type of lad, full of energy and fun. He chattered on and on about his animals: he had a sheep of his own who had lambed early. He had his small, friendly dog with him. His neighbour, the farmer, let him play amongst the cows and the horses. He showed her his toy: a roughly carved train made for him by his father. His mother had died last year but his father was proving an excellent parent. Although the ground was currently too hard to dig out the winter vegetables and the water had to be thawed so it could be used, the boy told her that he and his father had a jolly time at the station and in the station house.

This poor child, with his wise and kindly father, fascinated her, so happy with so little, able to extract joy from everyday living. As her toes warmed up, and the child prattled on, she began to relax. Then there was a hush: the draughts ceased, the world held its breath, and from the heavens came snow.

Huge soft flakes filled the air and covered the ground with white. The browns and the greys were hidden by the gift of beauty in the air. Fancifully, she imagined silent angels falling, dancing and sweeping through the atmosphere, and she and the boy went outside. As the snow kissed her skin, they danced in the new-made world. The boy sang, the station master joined in and Christina threw her head back and laughed.

Later, sitting alone now in the waiting room, she took up her notebook and wrote some lines:

In the bleak midwinter, frosty wind made moan,
Earth stood hard as iron, water like a stone.

Later, on the train, as it chugged towards London and home, she realised that the boy and his father, their love of each other and of their animals, their generosity and joy, in this hardest of times, were also gifts to her, and to any human being with the openness of heart to accept them. She finished her poem, and tucked it away in her reticule, unsure whether or not she would show it to anyone. It really didn't matter if no-one else ever read it, or saw it: it was enough that she had experienced it.

Lost

'That's it, I've had enough. I'm off. I'm leaving you.'

And with that, Claire stormed out of the new house. She had recently bought it with her husband and their relationship had not been the same since they moved from the flat. The house was ambitious, an architect-designed piece with a large garden: almost in its own grounds. They were both working hard, Claire at a very tedious job, to pay for it.

In her temper, Claire turned the wrong way, the way she used to turn when leaving the flat, and found herself in the back garden, facing the woods behind. It didn't matter, she used the momentum that her anger had given her and marched, fighting tears, to the gate in the fence.

Once through the fence and into the woods, Claire followed the footpath between the trees and bushes. However, before long, the path fizzled out and Claire realised that she was isolated. She thought about turning back, but was not, under any circumstances, going to tell Simon that she couldn't cope without him. Anyway, behind her, the bushes had closed in, burying the path. She had no choice but to move on, feeling her way into what now seemed like a forest.

Aware of creatures out of sight, but not out of earshot, she gathered any courage she might have, pulled her shoulders back, and began to regret her action. Something skittered near her left foot, and something pulled at her hair. Stifling a scream, she told herself that it was only a tree branch which she had shifted herself.

Having snagged her jacket on bushes - Claire had no idea what they were - she turned away from that direction, only to put her foot into a slimy patch, which might or might not have been bog, or a stream, or a decomposing body, or anything. 'Get a grip', she told herself.

Scraping the mud from her shoe, she plunged on, ever deeper into the forest, as night began to fall. Knowing that she was not far from home, she shouted. And shouted. And screamed. And cried. All sound was swallowed by the forest, and the dark. And the creatures could hear her.

Whimpering, she climbed onto the low branches of a tree, and tried to settle herself, but to no avail. The longest night of her life was eventually broken by a faint glimmer of light. Claire told herself that it was Simon coming with a torch to find her. Again, she shouted, and again, the sound was lost. The glimmer faded, and so she had to wait until dawn.

Dawn came, a dull, diffuse and murky dawn, darkened by fog. Dense fog that even hid the trees. Now hungry and dreadfully thirsty, Claire decided to turn back and deal with the consequences when she was safe. But, climbing down from her tree, she had no idea which direction was 'back'. The fog obscured any landmarks, even if bushes can be described as such. Instead, Claire pushed forward, in whichever direction that was. Again she found the slime, and decided to follow it, reasoning that it was most probably a stream. She remembered many years ago being told that if you are lost, follow a stream.

The muddy slime sucked at her shoes, and the water steadily became deeper, and faster. The sides of the stream were steeper, and the sound of rushing water louder. She slipped, and the water carried her deeper into the forest, deeper into the dark and the fog. Flailing, Claire grasped a branch which overhung the river, and with a monumental effort, pulled herself onto the bank.

Lost

For a second, the fog lifted and Claire glimpsed a vast open space, and realised that she had just saved herself from a disastrous end, tumbling down a waterfall. Moving forward, she gasped as she only just stopped her foot slipping on the edge of the cliff.

She was exhausted. She couldn't go back: she couldn't go forward. She curled up on the edge of the precipice, and cried. She realised how selfish she had been, rushing out in the middle of what now seemed a very silly argument about supper. How could a desire to go out to a restaurant have led to this? Simon had said he was tired and needed to work, and Claire said that she needed some excitement, something different. Well, she certainly had that. She realised how worried Simon must be, that he must be frantic. That he would not have been able to follow her as her path had been obscured.

Looking up, she took note of her surroundings: the first time since she had ran out on Simon. She was on a headland, with the river and precipice to her left, and a soft, green, undulating plain to her right. She became aware of a human voice, hailing her. Looking up, and across the plain before her she saw a man gesturing. He was waving, attracting her, inviting her. To her right was a path that led down the escarpment and onto the plain.

Stiff, tired, and conscience-stricken, she made her way towards the distant man. He was dressed in old gardening clothes, and was tending a small vegetable garden.

'I have water from my spring, and bread fresh from my oven. Please, eat,' said the man. 'How did you come to this place?'

'I don't know,' replied Claire. 'I just want to go home. I want to see Simon. I want him to know that I am sorry, that I seemed to be lost in my own needs, that I was stuck in my own head, being carried along by my egotism and that I was allowing our marriage to fall apart, to fall headlong into an abyss. I couldn't see what I was doing, and now I have forced myself into your peace and quiet.'

'But you are not uninvited, my dear,' he said. 'You were lost and needed help. No-one who needs help should find themselves uninvited anywhere.'

'But can I go home? How will I ever find my way back? Do you have any pearls of wisdom to help with that?'

'Yes, my dear. If it is pearls of wisdom you need, you must look within yourself, for there are the pearls that are your own knowledge. You must look within yourself with clarity, with perception and with honesty. It is not enough to demand, or to blame. Sleep now, and all will be well.' And she did. Refreshed by the sparkling clear water, and satisfied by the wholesome bread, she slept peacefully.

On awakening, the man's dwelling was gone, the plain had become a wood and Claire was sitting on a bench. The dappled sun shone through the birches and she could hear Simon.

'Claire, for god's sake, come back in, this is ridiculous. It's this house, it's too much; we need to be together on it or we'll never survive.' And he came through the back gate, sat next to her on the bench, and took her hand. 'I've ordered a curry, and dug out a dvd. Let's stay in, and I won't do any work tonight. Let's just be together.'

And Claire looked inside herself, and found that the pearl within was Simon.

The Departure

The sun slipped further down in the sky, throwing ever lengthening shadows over the trio trudging along the lane, making their way to the distant staging inn. The two men carried a box between them and the woman, tears threatening, bore a large basket. They walked silently, conversation subdued, for none of them could bear the answer another would give.

Reaching the Red Boar, the men gratefully stored the box in the luggage room, to await the arrival of the stagecoach in the early hours of the morning, and the three sad travellers settled in a quiet room which contained two large easy chairs and a large roaring log fire. The men settled themselves into the chairs and the woman sat on a stool at the feet of the younger man, barely more than a boy.

'Come, come, let us be of more cheer,' cried John, the older man. 'We are here to celebrate! Jem is not leaving us, he is off to take up a great offer. It is such an honour for someone from our village to be called to the Bar!'

'Hardly called to the Bar,' laughed Jem. But it is an honour, Sister, to be given a chance to study the law under the great Sir Joshua Braithwaite. It is true I will be working in the London Law Courts, but as a humble apprentice, not quite a barrister.'

'Yet,' cried his proud brother-in-law. But he noticed quiet tears stealing down the cheeks of his beloved wife. 'My dear, Jem will be well. He will be staying in the house of Sir Matthew, living in the great heart of the greatest city. His life will be full; it will be exciting; it will be successful. What chance does a bright young man have in our village, where even the priest must share parishes, and the stagecoach does not come?'

'But,' replied Sadie, quaveringly, 'will he have enough to eat? Will he have to work all his waking hours, and never have time to think of us?'

'Darling Sister, how could I ever forget you and your kindness? Since our dear mother died, you have been my little mother. But never forget how you encouraged me into ambition, to want more than the village can offer. This is the beginning of what you have worked for.'

A brave smile, a tiny sniff, a surreptitious wiping away of a tear. 'You are right, my Jem, let us celebrate with a jar of punch.'

And so, duly, a jar of punch was ordered, together with a supper of cold ham, pork pie, fresh bread and cheeses. John plunged the hot poker into the punch to heat it and all three partook heartily of their supper. Another jar of punch, and yet another.

Sadie rested her head on Jem's knee and slept and the two men talked through the night.

'She will be all right, won't she?' asked Jem who cared for his sister as much as she cared for him. 'You will make sure that you get the right midwife when her time comes? Please make sure that she is attended by Mrs. Geeson, who is the only midwife who manages to deliver children sober. And you will get help in to work the land after the laying in, because Sadie will be preoccupied and weak. If you try to work the land yourself, she will worry and will be trying to help you far too soon.'

'Jem, she is my wife. Of course I will care for her. And when our child arrives, you will be the first to know. If it is a boy, she wants to call him Jeremiah. And if a girl, Jeremina!'

The Departure

And so the night passed. Sadie slept fitfully, close to her brother and the two men explored their excitement, one looking to his life in London and the other the prospect of fatherhood. The each reassured the other of his best wishes and of their care for Sadie.

At five o'clock, when the world was still dark, and the fire burned low, and the punch was all gone, the boy came into the room with breakfast. Again, conversation was difficult, and none knew how to say goodbye. No member of their family had ever left the village before. Breakfast was difficult, and no-one could eat much, but the porter helped to maintain some semblance of spirit.

Outside, the clatter of horses and carriage wheels sounded and the men stood. John oversaw Jem's box being stored safely under the carriage as he and Sadie said their farewells.

'I have brought this basket, dear Jem, with food for your journey. And a muffler to keep you warm, for I know how you do not think of such things. Please, my dear, write regularly, eat properly, keep well and avoid all of the criminal elements.'

Deciding not to remind her that his position involved dealing exactly with criminal elements, he reassured her that he would follow every word of her advice, and with a final hug, he leapt into the seat alongside the driver. Jem's heart was heavy for leaving his sister in her family state, but, as the coach readied to leave, his young heart sung at the prospect of a shining adventure.

As the day began to break, the coach set off with a cheery hail from all passengers, as Sadie and John waved it away.

John placed his arm around his wife's waist and led her along the path towards the sunrise, towards their home, their cosy home with comfortable furniture, ample food, and an equally shining future full of sons and daughters of their own.

Coming Home

The queue stretched seemingly for miles, snaking away into the dark. She shivered, and he put his arms around her, protectively, keeping her safe from the cold, the uncertain wait. To the side, the deep shadows of the locked church, bells silenced, loomed with hidden horrors waiting in the overgrown black shrubs, trembling in the cutting wind.

Wearing only a light jacket and high-heeled shoes, she hadn't expected this. In her naivety, she had expected only a night out, a meal with friends. But the memory of that time faded in her anxiety of what awaited at journey's end. He stood by her, sympathetic, loving, his strong masculine arms creating a barrier between her and the future.

But she knew that they must, at some point, part. That he must go on to his own destined arrival, and that she must face hers alone.

The queue shuffled forwards, slowly, as time passed and the night breeze blew ever colder. Her feet hurt in her light party shoes as she buried her face in his chest, warm, supportive, his own particular smell enveloping her, giving some comfort, some warmth, some belief.

Vehicles arrived singly, in convoys, taking people into the night to wherever they were going. Pushed by those behind and the officer in control, no time was lost as couples, groups, singles were hustled into the dark vehicles, engines idling, impatient to be moving.

The streetlights suddenly extinguished, throwing the area into total darkness. The looming shadows of the closed church grew, overwhelmed the world. The wind blew stronger, colder in the darkness, the shrubs rustled their secrets and her flimsy clothing highlighted her vanity, the unrealistic belief that she would not need to prepare for all possibilities. She had defied common sense so many times in the past, getting away with it. But this time, this night, with unexpected inevitability, her insouciance failed and she was having to face her new reality.

The umbrous head of the queue was lit only by single approaching vehicle, arriving to shuttle the next waiting, shivering, passengers to their journey's end. But, steadily, so slowly, the queue moved forward. Strangely, no-one communicated. There was no desire to speak to those equally trapped, to hear their stories of woe, of being trapped in this place, unexpectedly caught in this eventuality. Instead, people turned inwards, silently, holding each other for warmth and security, huddling in pairs, fours. People had even stopped looking at their watches. Time became meaningless, and watch faces black.

And then, after a seemingly eternal wait, watching the queue grow shorter, they reached their turn. They stood at the head of the queue for some time, the officer making unwelcome jokes, and her fear becoming more and more acute. Their vehicle arrived. They were ushered in, with great haste and little ceremony. They were whisked off into the night.

He held her ever tighter. She assured him that she would be fine on her own, that her fear was silly, that she could cope with anything that would happen. He held her more, kissed her face tenderly, as if for the last time, and their eyes met, with love, even in the darkness of the vehicle.

They arrived. Well, she arrived. Alighting the vehicle alone, she once more reassured him. As he was taken away into the darkness of the night, she faced the building rising up before her at the end of a pathway. As she tentatively began her solitary, cold, apprehensive walk towards the building, the door flew open and she heard a voice bark sharply from the man silhouetted in the shaft of light glaring through the door.

'In here. Now. Don't argue or even try to excuse yourself. Just get in.'

She dropped her head, as if in apology, shuffled down the rest of the path, reluctantly approaching her trial, unjust as it was.

'Where the hell have you been? Your mother is going out of her mind. Twelve o'clock we said, and now it's after two. And I have to be in work at eight. If that's the respect he shows us, you can finish with him right now, young lady.'

The Mirror

There was a delivery, an unexpected delivery. A box about twenty-four inches square but only about five inches high. 'Fragile' was stamped on the parcel. Doris opened it carefully, and inside was a mirror, a convex mirror, of the sort she had had above the mantelpiece when she was newly married. She had no idea where it had come from, but it was delightful nevertheless. She asked the young man next door if he would hang it up for her.

Once up, Doris loved it. She loved the wide view of her comfortable living room, with her chair to the left, and the fireside rug in the centre. She enjoyed looking in it whenever she passed it. Somehow, it made the room look tidier and fresher than it really was. The nets over the balcony windows seemed whiter, newer.

On Tuesday morning, as she checked her familiar reflection, now slightly distorted, she was aware of a flicker behind the curtains. Checking the balcony, she assured herself that the door was locked and the balcony empty.

However, that evening, the flicker returned, and to her surprise, there was a child standing in the mirror, in front of her reflection. He was about four years old, unfamiliar, but smiling, waving as if he knew her. She told herself not to be silly and busied herself making her tea, trying to put both the boy and the flicker behind the curtains out of her mind.

The next day, the child was still there, and Doris was sure she heard him giggle. A warm, life-affirming giggle: in the mirror, not in the room. Shaking her head, Doris realised she had been asleep, dozing in the armchair, not looking in the mirror at all. She made a sandwich and turned on the television.

The Mirror

During the next few days, Doris tried to avoid the mirror, as it was not having a good effect on her. However, she did need to check her hair before she went out to do her shopping. This time there was a young family in the mirror, looking and waving at her, smiling, beckoning. She knew none of these people: not the three children, of whom the boy was one, not the happy young couple, clearly the parents of the children. Not even the middle-aged, balding man standing behind them.

But there was something about him. A look in his eyes, a cast of the mouth, the angle of the chin. She didn't know him, she was clear about that, but he seemed to know her. And at the back of her head, deep inside her brain she heard a single word, 'Mum'.

She hadn't heard that word used to describe herself since that terrible day when eleven-year-old Keith had been knocked down: the day that not only his life ended. But there, in her head was his word, his voice, his warmth. She would recognise it to her last day. And the curtains flickered.

'Are you all right, love?' said the kind woman sitting next to her. Doris was confused, but found herself sitting on a bus, nearing her stop: she had dropped off again. She assured the woman that she had only been napping, and left the bus, overwhelmed with loneliness and loss, of a kind she hadn't felt in years.

Returning home, she unpacked her shopping and prepared to tackle the washing up from breakfast. However, she decided to allow herself a couple of minutes in her chair, with a nice cup of tea and a chocolate digestive, to cheer herself up and properly come to.

However, despite all her resolution, she found herself looking in the mirror again, this time hoping to see the family, particularly the middle-aged man who seemed so real. They were all there, together with others, a big, extended family: loving, together, united. Doris put her hand out to the mirror, and the surface shimmered. She could have sworn that she felt the touch of one of the children and lip-read 'Nanna' through his grin.

That was enough, it was all she could take. She took a step forward, and entered the mirror. At once, they all surrounded her, with hugs, laughter, warmth, familiar voices: her soul soared as she felt a sense of belonging and the joy of being with the family that she had never had.

And the curtains flickered. And out stepped her beloved Albert, so long gone. And here, as if he had always been here, as if they had never been separated.

As he folded her in his arms, and the wash of his love overwhelmed her, she looked back. And as she did, she saw the mirror, as it started to fog, to cloud, beginning to obscure the lonely room, and herself lying back in her chair, a smile resting on her lifeless features.

Moving On

The old town and the Cathedral complex had been a lot closer than she thought. And the weather better. A warm sun smiled down although it could get perhaps a little strong when it moved around to the back of her head. She smiled. That would be hours yet. She'd have moved on long before then. There was a stone bench set into the boundary wall of the great cathedral. She took a seat with her back to the cathedral and facing the monastery of St. Martin, allowing space for the attractive young couple holding hands and whispering, their heads inclined closely towards each other.

A bell chimed twice. A medium sized, slightly flat, metallic chime calling the half hour: one for the quarter, two for the half, three to get ready... and go cat go. Thoughts uncontrolled, she smiled inwardly, enjoying her private joke.

The elated mood stemmed from the service she had just attended. The Pilgrims' Mass in the church dedicated to Santiago, Saint James, apostle and apparently the purpose of the third most important Christian pilgrimage after Jerusalem and Rome. Not a catholic, not even particularly a Christian, she was a dedicated traveller and terminally curious: she had been to all of those places and even partaken in a service in each of them. She had enjoyed this one. A list of places that today's pilgrims had originated from followed by music, prayers, and finally, the *botafumeiro*, the great censer itself swung across the transept, filling the space with a deep smoky incense. There had been a ripple of excitement as the vergers untied the ropes, and a swathe of cameras were raised by people now uncaring about the 'no pictures' exhortation, including her own. She had not partaken of the communion, ruefully remembering the reaction of her committed Roman Catholic friend in St. Peter's in Rome when she had thought she might like to try.

After the service she had joined the queue to view the saint's tomb and, while queueing, had seen a notice inviting people to 'embrace the apostle' and of course she had joined that queue as well, never one to pass an opportunity by. The queue had snaked around the apse, through a gate and up some extremely worn stairs. At the top, she found herself behind the statue of St. James himself which stood over the high altar. And she followed the lead of those in front of her and dutifully embraced the statue, putting her hands on his shoulders and bowing her head. Naughty thoughts about idolatry had been quashed as she reminded herself that she was a guest and a visitor.

The sound of people approaching caught her attention and brought her back to the present. This spot was the last bit before pilgrims entered the *Obradorio,* the cathedral square, and approaching was a large group of young people, walking three abreast. It became obvious that the person in the centre of each trio was blind. There was no indication of how far they had walked, but clearly they had come further than she had.

Until then, she was happy that she had chosen to do her 'pilgrimage' her way: 'fly in, drink a lot of Albariño and fly out again'. But the sight of these young people, either disabled or guiding them, struck a chord in her lazy heart. Nevertheless the sight pleased her, and as usual, any feeling of guilt wafted away like a shadow passing the sun.

The square was quiet again. A distant sound of a wailing bagpipe (apparently Galician as well) underscored the quiet conversation of people passing by. The slightest hint of a suggestion of a breath of a breeze filled the air with the scent of tulips, blooming in the garden of the monastery of St, Martin, giving colour and delicacy to the imposing façade.

The bell sounded three times.

Moving On

Taking out a tangerine filched from the breakfast buffet, she peeled it and turned her attention to her kindle, and the next chapter of a crime novel, totally indistinguishable from a thousand others. She wasn't even sure if she had read this one before or not (she had).

Unable to concentrate on the forensic details of a fictional murder, her mind wandered again to the coffee she had enjoyed that morning on the other side of the cathedral under an umbrella in the open air. A very strange thing had been a musician with an electric guitar playing old Andy Williams hits: *Can't Take my Eyes off You* and *Love Story*. (How her teenaged self had loved that film!) But the odd thing was that the musician was wearing a black balaclava with the mouth cut out, and black gloves with the fingertips cut off. He looked like a black minstrel. Hmmm. Not sure how that would go down in sensitive Britain: she had surreptitiously filmed him for posterity.

An elderly gentleman caught her attention by nodding to her as he sat on the bench at the other end from the young couple, still oblivious to anything but each other. She wriggled up, so English, ensuring that there was equal personal space between everyone on the bench.

Pilgrims continued to arrive, in long, trailing groups all dressed in pink tee shirts or identified by yellow scarves. Or in smaller groups, all happy, elated to be at journey's end. For the most part they were quiet, contemplating arrival, or exhausted after the long trek. Some photographed the cathedral, some each other. A few, a very few, whooped with delight.

Tourists were different. In huge flocks led by their shepherd, or independents in twos or fours, they were all louder, announcing their presence, photographing everything, examining selfies with a fervour that matched that of the earlier Mass. And discussing lunch.

And then, without warning, the square was empty. Just those silent few on the stone bench. Even the bagpiper had stopped. And the bell rang four times. And it was followed by the belly-deep boom of the great cathedral clock tolling the hour. Three times it reverberated the air, turning space, pale tulips and grand old buildings into aspects of sound alone.

As the last deep boom died away, she became aware of life returning to the space. People talking, and the sun, having arced in the sky, was burning the back of her neck. A man with a guitar set up an amplifier and occupied the square with incompetent busking. She put away the almost forgotten kindle, gathered up the tangerine peelings, nodded to the elderly gentleman at the end of the bench and went in search of a glass of wine. Time to move on.

Aliens Averted

Charley was bored out of his mind. The Geography lesson just went on and on and on. He'd finished reading the page, making the notes, colouring in the map. Everyone else seemed to be still at it but for Charley it seemed that time had stood still.

He looked out of the window; he wrote his initials on the desk; he pinged paper pellets at the boy in front; he pulled faces at the teacher. No-one noticed a thing and no-one reacted to anything.

But, suddenly, out of the corner of his eye, Charley saw movement. A spider, a big spider with hairy legs and a big fat body came crawling in through the open window. Charley's heart sang: finally, some fun. He crept his left hand across the window ledge and caught the spider by one of its muscular legs.

'Oi,' he heard, from outside the window. 'Put me down.' Intrigued, Charley looked out of the window, and there, to his utter amazement, he saw Spiderman hanging down with his leg caught on the windowsill.

'You're Spiderman,' said Charley, his interest finally captured.

'Oh, really? And what makes you think that?' snapped Spiderman. 'Could it be the red spandex, or maybe the giant spider emblazoned across my chest?'

'No need to be sarky,' said Charley. 'I wasn't exactly expecting you to turn up to my Geography lesson.'

'Ok, enough talking,' said Spiderman. 'We've got work to do. I'm here to get your superpowers. There is an alien invasion about to happen in the centre of town and we have got to stop it. Look sharp, lad.'

'But I don't have any special powers. What can I do to stop an alien invasion? Are you sure you've got the right person?'

'Yes,' replied Spiderman, testily. 'Otherwise I wouldn't be here, would I, duh? Come on! Stop wasting time talking. And while you're about it, let go of my leg.'

And with barely a glance at his teacher, Charley followed Spiderman out through the window and stood on the ledge. Thor was standing there.

'At last. You two do talk. Come on, whatever your name is, grab this hammer, we have to get moving.' And with that, Thor grabbed Charley around the waist and they flew through the sky, powered by Thor's mighty hammer.

They landed just outside the Tesco Metro. Iron Man was there, tapping his foot impatiently and looking at his superwatch.

'Right, this is the plan. The aliens are due to arrive in two and a half minutes. Thor, you take Spidey and the lad up to the roof of the multi-storey and wait for me. I'll fetch Bruce Banner and we'll join you. Once we are there, we will have about ninety seconds before the aliens arrive. As soon as we can see them, I want you, boy, to do your stuff. Then Spidey can web them so they can't move; Thor and myself will go around the back to attack and Bruce, by then, will be so angry, he will have Hulked. Once we are all in place, we'll just go in for the kill. Spidey, have you got the necessary?'

'Yup.'

And within seconds, pulled into the sky by Thor's hammer, Charley found himself standing on the deserted roof of the multi-storey. Instantly, Thor and Ironman zoomed off into the atmosphere, moving so quickly that it was as if they had disappeared.

'Hello, Bruce,' said Spidey to a mild looking man who was leaning quietly against the fence. 'How are you feeling? Have you got the stuff to help the boy?'

'Yes, of course. I am a physics expert, you know, not just a Hulk. Ok, then, I suppose we'd better start.'

And with that, Bruce Banner handed Charley a Physics book and told him to turn to page 36, read the chapter and copy out the diagrams onto the graph paper in the back. Charley, of course, was too afraid of Bruce Banner to argue. He thought that any arguing, sass or time wasting might bring the wrath of the Incredible Hulk upon him.

So he simply said, 'Yes, sir.' And got on with it. He stifled a sigh, a yawn and tried to stop his shoulders from slumping as he reluctantly opened the boring book, picked up the boring pencil and turned to boring page 36.

And at that moment, the aliens arrived. Screaming out of the sky, with guns ready and pointed, in a giant ship bound directly for Charley's home town, the aliens arrived.

But Charley had Physics to do. And at that moment, at precisely that moment, his superpower kicked in. Total, absolute, irredeemable boredom. Time stopped. The world stopped turning, the aliens were suspended above the car park, shoppers halted in their errands, traffic came to a standstill and only the superheroes could move.

Within seconds, Spiderman had covered the aliens in his superweb which held them still in case Charley inadvertently found the Physics interesting. Thor pulled the aliens out of their spaceship; Ironman drove it away from the earth and exploded it in the stratosphere. Bruce Banner Hulked and grabbed the aliens, and Hulksmashed them until they pleaded for mercy.

The superheroes all returned, job done. Ironman spoke for them all. 'It's ok, you can stop doing the Physics now, Boredomboy. We couldn't have done it without you. The earth will be forever grateful to you.'

And, said Bruce Banner, no longer the Hulk, 'When you have passed all your exams, you can join us as a full-blown Avenger. Thor and Spidey, take him back, please and then we'll take these aliens to a secure site somewhere in the Galaxy where no-one will ever find them.'

As Charley was delivered back to his classroom, Spidey said goodbye and added, 'We mean it, you know. Yours is a very special power, but use it carefully.'

Charley settled back into his seat and looked wistfully out of the window, wondering if he would ever see his new friends, or use his superpower ever again.

And finally, his teacher noticed. 'Charley, will you please stop staring out of that window. What are you looking for, aliens?'

The Time of Your Life

'Thank you so much for taking part in our experiment, Dr Palmer.'

'It's so intriguing, I couldn't resist. And please call me Jane. Could you explain a bit more, please?'

'Well, we're trialling a memory technique. It should feel very much like time travel, but actually you will be revisiting your memory. We attach electrodes to you head, and sensors to the rest of you, just to keep check. Then we put you into a deep REM sleep and record the brain waves. The important part is that you are completely open and honest with us about what you experience when you debrief with the counsellor afterwards. We are hoping to send you to the best moment of your life and, believe me, some people's best moments are somewhat surprising. The ultimate purpose, of course, is that we will be able to pinpoint a moment and take people back, for therapeutic purposes. At this experimental stage, we are aiming for the best moment, mostly to encourage volunteers.'

'How wonderful. I wonder what it will be? My wedding day? That moment in Machu Picchu? My sixth birthday party? My eighteenth? Something really embarrassing? I can't wait.'

And with that, she lay on the bed, had the electrodes attached and something was injected into her wrist. She instantly fell into a deep sleep......

It was a drizzly November night. The staff in the office were all going out to say goodbye to one of their colleagues. Bob had been the only one there, really, with any sense of fun and Jane would miss him. He was holding the do in his local, a dingy place near a housing estate. He had asked them to put on snacks and give everyone a drink on him. Then they were on their own.

Jane had been looking forward to the evening, expecting Bob to play some sort of silly game or maybe some practical jokes. But no such luck.

The men all sat around the bar, drinking pint after pint, getting loudly and uproariously drunk while the women sat around a table, nursing martini and lemonades or whisky and gingers. Jane wanted to get drunk, to join the men at the bar, and to laugh with Bob before he disappeared over the horizon.

But instead, she sat at the table, picking at a dispiriting bowl of damp crisps and trying to make her warm white wine last. The women, apart from Jane, were animated. One of them was in the process of moving house, into her first real home with her new husband. She was excited about choosing furniture and the others were more than happy to help. They discussed curtains. Should the curtain lining be the same upstairs and down, so the house presents a uniform front to the street? Should the nets face in or out? Should the lamp shades tone or contrast with the curtains and carpet? And the kitchen: curtains or blinds? Should the shower curtain be discreet, dramatic or fun? And the bedroom rugs: sheepskins, plain or patterned? They were all so excited.

This went on for some hours, until someone decided they had had enough fun and it was time to escape, or as they called it 'go home'. Jane got home to find Dave fast asleep on the sofa, in his underpants, and surrounded by empty beer cans. The television was still on.

She sighed deeply, left him to it, and went to bed……..

And awoke into a laboratory. 'How was it?' was the first question.

'I thought you said it would be the time of my life. It was probably the most miserable evening I've ever had. I'm looking forward to seeing how the counsellor deals with this one.

And the counsellor did. After long sessions with doctors, psychiatrists, and scientists, they finally found out how their new drug had sent Jane to such an apparently innocuous, uninspiring moment.

The report said: Doctor Jane Palmer (subject), a volunteer for the 'Time of Your Life' Project, had apparently disappointing results. However, that particular moment was finally revealed as pivotal to the rest of her life. After this event, she asserted herself and the following occurred:

1. She gave up smoking *not a necessarily direct correlation, but her first act of self-determination.*
2. She told Dave to leave and insisted upon it. *The assertion at this point is quite remarkable.*
3. She enrolled at the University to obtain academic qualifications.
4. She left the office.
5. She achieved a first-class degree, and went on to obtain her Doctorate.
6. She married her tutor.
7. The travelled the world, for research purposes, to attend conferences and for diversion.
8. They raised 2 sons and 2 daughters.
9. She retired in order to devote herself to medical research.

On receiving the report, Jane went back to the laboratory. She fully accepted that that evening was, indeed 'the time of her life', but there were questions. The first was how the drug induced her mind to such a deep analysis even before its application. This was something that had to be investigated, perhaps even before the research proceeded. Clearly the drug worked but there had to be control on how it worked before it could be administered to genuinely vulnerable patients. Secondly, they had to work out what sort of drug it was: a memory enhancer, a truth drug, or hallucinogen which causes the brain to analyse itself. If the last, it would open up a whole new area of research.

But, Jane was happy to concur, that the evening in the pub was indeed 'the time of her life' because without it, she would still be in some office, in some flat, with some bloke, and wondering what she had done with her life. They had told her that some results were surprising.

The Wall

I was on my way back from the supermarket. I'd run out of bread and thought I'd get in some supplies. I was thinking about what I would wear to the party that night when something caught my attention on the radio and made me laugh. As I did, my foot slipped on the accelerator and I ran into a low garden wall. The wall couldn't have been very good because it completely crumbled.

I jumped out of the car as a woman came running out of the house. I apologised profusely and gave her my contact and insurance details, assuring her that I would pay for any repairs. She was probably delighted because that wall seriously needed looking at. Anyway, there was very little damage to the car. The wing was a bit bent and the nearside light would need replacing but it was fine to drive, at least to the garage.

As I left the garage, carrying my shopping, the mechanic called me back. 'Hey mate, don't forget your gnome,' he laughed, and handed me a garden gnome. It was about twelve inches tall, with a smiley face, a cute red hat and he was holding a flower.

'Not mine,' I replied.

'Well, it was on your passenger seat,' he said, as he tucked it under my arm.

Once I was on the bus, I had a good look at it. The cute smile hardened and the eyes glittered. 'You murdered me,' he said.

I don't know how I heard him because I am sure he didn't speak aloud. I answered, sotto voce, that I hadn't.

'You dropped a wall on me. I am crushed to dust. I can never be repaired.'

91

I left it on the bus. Put it down to shock. Got home and got ready for the party. It was my mate, Jimmy's promotion party and we were going to get him hammered.

We met in the Crown and began, as custom dictates, with a couple of tequila slammers all round. It was as I downed the second that I noticed the gnome on the table in front of Jimmy.

'You murdered me,' he hissed.

I suggested we move onto The Lamb and we did.

That night I slept fitfully. Probably because I'd had too much to drink, but I dreamed about the gnome. And what a dream. There were about six gnomes. Their blank smiles hiding tiny, pointed teeth. Their button eyes bearing gleams of malice and accusation. I woke up shouting, 'I'm sorry. I didn't do it on purpose. It was an accident...'

But the thought persisted. 'You killed our friend.

I got through the day, expecting to see malevolent gnomes everywhere. It wasn't until I was in the pub after work with some colleagues that the first gnome tapped me on the shoulder. 'You murdered me,' he spat.

'Did you say something?' asked Gerry. Clearly the gnome could be heard.

'Yes,' I replied. 'I'll have a double. And then I had another. And eventually I managed to shut the gnome out, even though he and his friends persisted.

It was when I was on my way home that if felt the first sting on my ankle. I turned in time to see a gnome with a fishing rod gesturing triumphantly that he had snagged my ankle and torn

The Wall

my jeans. There were about a dozen of them, all casting their hooks at my legs.

'This is our chance!' one shouted. All of us who have been broken or damaged by thoughtless human beings. Now is our time.'

I have to admit, I was terrified. I started to run but I could feel fishing hooks tearing my clothes and into my flesh. I jumped over a gate but they easily passed through it. Those with flower pots started pelting me with earth and other kinds of filth. Those with wheelbarrows produced missiles which stung and tore at my skin, allowing the filth to gather in the wounds. A baying crowd of sharp-toothed, vengeful gnomes were in pursuit, each bent on tearing the clothes from my back and scarring my flesh. I threw a shoe at the crowd: I had no other weapon. I ripped off my filthy clothing and threw it behind me, in an attempt to slow them down.

I fled through the garden behind the gate, came to a door and entered, without any thought but to escape the hissing, howling, snapping mob, bent on exacting revenge on just one heedless human.

They couldn't pass through the glass but they pressed themselves against the windows, countless numbers of them, their bland plaster smiles distorted into images of hatred and horror as they waited, patiently, gleefully, murderously, for me to leave.

I crawled into a space in the corner, cowering into the shadows where they could no longer find me. And I thought that I would stay there, safe, hidden for ever, and fall into a sleep so deep that I would never awaken. The safe darkness closed around me. But I heard a scream. I didn't know if it was mine; I couldn't tell if it had emanated from my consciousness or another's. It seems it had come from a woman.

And that, your honour, is why I was drunk, naked and hiding behind a pot plant in a stranger's conservatory.

The Princess and the Frog

Well, there I was, sunning myself on the edge of the pond, watching the little'uns playing and enjoying a bit of croak with my old mate, Kermit. Suddenly, a hand grabbed me from above and whooshed me through the air, and a big face planted a huge, slobbery kiss right on the top of my head. Well, I ask you, that's sexual assault for a start.

Then she had the audacity to say, 'You were supposed to turn into a prince. What's the matter with you?'

'With ME?' I shouted. 'What's the matter with YOU?'

And she plopped me right down on the edge of the pond and picked up Kermit and did the exact same thing to him.

And with that, she threw her golden ball into the pond and stomped off, shouting, 'Stupid frogs.'

Well the ball was a bit of a nuisance because it had stunned all the fish and terrified the young'uns. And I suppose it meant that she'd be back to get it.

She did come back later and picked up both me and Kermit, looked closely, and I may say, a little intimately. She put him back and stuck a stupid little crown on my head. 'You'll do,' she announced, as if there was an audience.

And then she kidnapped me and took me into the palace. Right into her room we went, and she plonked me down on her pillow. It was silk and a bit slippery. I had to keep wriggling around to stop myself falling off. But she made me a nice little velvet cushion to sit on with a nice little velvet cape to match.

Anyway, long story short, we both calmed down a bit and she explained that she had been told about an enchanted prince who had been turned into a frog. She wasn't sure if a, I was the right frog, or b, she knew how to break the enchantment. She had thought a kiss would do it. After all, it worked for those princes who had to wake up princesses in thorny thickets and glass cases. But it hadn't worked with me. So she had looked up the enchantment in the palace library. There were several remedies. There was the kiss one that hadn't worked. Then there was the throwing the golden ball into the pond one, and that hadn't worked either. The other one seemed to be that she had to throw me against the wall.

Well, as you can imagine, I was dead against that one, mostly because it would have rendered me dead, enchantment or no. But by that time, we had got to quite like each other and she agreed that throwing me against the wall was probably not the best thing to do.

She took me to meet her father, who was, I admit, hoping for someone a bit more, well, humanish, but she said how much she liked me. He wasn't entirely happy but he did suggest that perhaps I could metamorphose into a prince. He said that I had already changed from a tadpole so one more metamorphosis couldn't be that difficult. I told him that I wasn't keen and that I could make the same case out about the princess changing into a frog. She was a spoiled brat really, and stamped her pretty foot and insisted that I was her soul mate, other half, the one. The poor man stood no chance: he had no choice but to give his permission.

I'm glad we held out because we've been together now for getting on fifty years. Yup, our golden wedding is coming up and the populace are preparing all sorts of celebratory parties and things. I've been king now for about twenty-five years and we seem to be doing okay. She's still a spoiled brat, but she's kind and she'll do for me. The great-grandchildren are starting to arrive now, some of them tadpoles and some of them babies. But we both love them all, there's no speciesism in our family.

But I have to admit, that there are times when I want to get away from the hurly-burly, and the servants and, yes, the stupid little gold crowns. So when Her Maj is off opening a hospital or inspecting a factory or collecting flowers from little girls, I slip off back to the old pond. Kermit is still there and we still have a bit of croak while watching the young'uns play.

The golden ball is still there. Nothing much has changed. It's been a good life, really.

The SS Orcades

A few days into the new year, 1961, the Orcades sailed from sunny Sydney bound for damp Tilbury, carrying a young family beset by failure and separation.

Derek and Barbara had tried, they really had. Ten pound poms, they had sought to make a new life for themselves and their two young daughters. But they had hit every problem that existed for immigrants to Australia: loss of employment, loss of housing, ill-health (and of course, with no work, there was no health insurance), and crippling home-sickness. Finally, living in a trailer park, they had asked for help.

The family in England had pulled together and saved enough to pay the return fare for Barbara and the girls. Derek would have to stay on and find work, any work, to save for his own fare and, hopefully, some capital to set up once home.

And so, Barbara, still only 27, said a temporary farewell to Derek in Brisbane, and, ashamed and defeated, led the girls onto the train to Sydney and then to their cabin: their home for the next four weeks.

But for six-year-old Sue, it was the beginning of an adventure that would shape her life. While Barbara wept, and the baby wailed, Sue could not help but be thrilled by the tickertape farewell from Sydney. As the great vessel pulled slowly, and noisily, away from the quay, the crowds threw ribbons and tape of all colours to the ship. And the passengers on the ship responded with their own.

A couple of days later, the same thing happened in Melbourne, then Adelaide and finally, Perth. As the ship was leaving Australia from Fremantle, the send-off was all the more excited. The tickertape, the brass bands, the hooting of the ship, the cheering and waving. The optimistic Aussie soul was at odds with Barbara's. Still, Derek would be home soon, and at least she would be safe. She had negotiated her way onto the ship, settled the girls into the cabin and was on her way to sanctuary.

And so the Orcades began her long journey from Fremantle to Suez. The ship settled into a routine and Sue felt all the freedom that can be felt by a six year old. She suffered from no sea-sickness; she revelled in the irony that was a swimming pool on a ship which was on the sea; she looked forward to the 10 o'clock ice cream, served to every child; she enjoyed the films shown in the afternoons; she explored the ship from prow to stern, from top to bottom, often returned to her concerned mother by a steward who had caught her somewhere she was not supposed to go. She particularly liked sneaking into the first class areas. She won the fancy dress competition, dressed as a Christmas cracker. One evening, when Barbara was at dinner, and Jacky was crying, Sue took three-year-old Jacky on a tour of the ship, ending up outside the dining room to catch Barbara coming out. Barbara was not best pleased. And so life took on a new perspective and ship-board living became normal.

And then, suddenly, things changed. The ship steamed into Aden. While waiting for clearance for the canal, the sea around seethed with tender boats, with all sorts of treasures for sale: hats, bright clothing, toys (especially stuffed camels), brilliant sparkling trinkets designed to imprint themselves on the memory of any curious six-year-old.

And then the canal. Desert on both sides, a horizon that was all sand rather than all water, the thrill of a different world. A world that, when they reached Port Said, became oh so real. They disembarked at Port Said. It was hot, dusty, crowded. The noise and the bustle, the smell of strange lands, with their camels and donkeys, their colourful spices and inviting foods (which she was NOT allowed to try). It was here that Barbara bought her a small leather stuffed camel, which she kept for ever.

And they were into the Mediterranean. The swimming pool was closed (too cold, apparently) to Sue's disappointment. The ship took on an air of expectation, a rustle of arrival was tangible. The air was noticeably cooler, but the atmosphere was one of warmth and promise.

One more stop: at Tunis, they again disembarked but Barbara couldn't cope with two small children in the heaving crowds in the port. Gibraltar was not a stop, but they saw they great rock, which guards the Mediterranean, from the side of the ship. The sight of Gibraltar made Barbara weep, for the first time since Fremantle. Sue assumed it was because it was so big, but Barbara explained that it somehow meant journey's end.

It wasn't, but there were no more stops. Only the White Cliffs of Dover, a few hours from Tilbury, heralded arrival. And at Tilbury, at journey's end, the homecoming. All three fell into the waiting and loving arms of the family who had gone without to bring the three of them home.

Sue saw snow that winter, and went to school in a different country. Derek came home six months later and the family were reunited.

And, presumably, the Orcades sailed back to Gibraltar, to Suez, to Fremantle and to Sydney. And the family settled, but six-year-old Sue became seven-year-old Sue and eventually adult Sue, who still needs the thrill of far-off places, glamorous destinations and onward travel. But she also needs to come home, to those she loves and those who love her. To those who wait, patiently, for her arrival from her exotic travels.

The Most Influential Relative

'Oh, my, god. I can't believe it! Me? Best actress? An Oscar? Oh just thank you, thank you, thank you everyone.

Look, I know I'm supposed to keep it short, but this is my moment, and I'm going to take it. I want to thank everyone, yes, everyone.

First, to my wonderful director, who was so patient and kind. And never minded when I needed to stay in my trailer with a headache instead of sitting at his side. And the cinematographer, my lovely cinematographer, who does not need to be named, who worked so hard to make me look authentic, to discover the truth of my role, while still making me look lovely. And of course, a shoutout to my wonderful team of hairdressers, dressers, make up and personal trainer. And the rest of my team: my lawyer, accountant, publicist who lets me interact with fans so well, and my security team who ensure those interactions are safe for us all.

Especially when I am doing my charity work, among the homeless and destitute of Los Angeles. Then my publicist and security work with my photographic team to ensure my heartfelt message gets out to everyone, and that the help that these poor people need is advertised across all the media.

And then of course is my fabulous family. My mama, who works so hard in her PR job, mingling, mixing, circulating and networking all hours of the day and night. She doesn't even really like partying, but she does it for the family. And she arranges so many dinner parties, and deals with so many wonderful Hollywood people when they visit our home.

My marvellous Daddy. Bless you, my love. There he is, in the front row. Give him the biggest applause, please. He deserves

101

it. As a producer, management consultant and general all-round good guy, he has led many film companies, and has poured all of his hard-earned money into his business. Where would any of us be without the investment and expertise of lovely men like him.

I know it's not fashionable to be proud of your brother, but mine is amazing. He is my personal manager. And he oversees everything I have been talking about. Without him I would be entirely lost. He organises and controls my brand. He gives me a reason to work and the commitment to succeed.

And let's not forget my grandad. Many of you will remember him from his own films back in the eighties. He worked on many, many productions, and is still working. Dear old grandad, who encouraged me to enter the business in the first place and paid for my training, my SAG membership, and my, let's be honest here, nose and boob jobs. And a little butt lift, and other tiny adjustments. Grandad, who used to be famous for how many girl friends he had, give him a cheer.

Of course, he always treated them all with respect and decency. None of that sordid stuff for him. He always ensured they were old enough and fully willing. And he only invited them to his hotel room if there was nowhere else available for their screen tests.

And it was grandad who introduced me to my loyal and lovely agent. He first cast me in one of Grandad's films. And I was lucky enough to work with Tom Hanks, as an ingénue. It wasn't a very big role but Tom Hanks introduced me to Stephen. And Mr. Spielberg said that I was good enough to stand on my own talent and that his friendship with Mama was totally nothing to do with casting.

I loved working with Sandra Bulloch, in our wacky police partnership film, and it was good to be able to show that I didn't have to be dependent on men. That's not a good look these days, is it? Dear Marty Scorsese cast me as a rape victim, which gave me a chance to act on behalf of all those victims of the male hierarchy. My part in the Me Too movement.

Of course, my superhero part in Marvel was like winning a prize all by itself. And so lovely to be able to work so closely with the man I was involved with then, especially as he was a person of colour. And one of my Daddy's closest friends.

But then came this film. A small-budget, independent film. It was wonderful to be able to take part in a project like this, and to bring my name to it to help finance it. The producer said that I even brought in Daddy's money. Wow.

But, it was hard. I had to search deep into my most private and precious emotions to be able to bring this part to you. To play an ordinary woman, living in Santa Monica, working in a bank, and raising two children. I don't know how women like her manage. Just as well she has a supportive husband. It was an unthought of privilege to enter the struggles and worries of such a life. And to read in my uncle's paper that 'being a truly ordinary woman is my finest and most testing performance' was overwhelming.

So, being trusted with this role was just the best. And to be given the best actress Oscar for it, well wow.

But most of all, I would like to thank my Auntie May. When I was small, I would go to stay with her and she always made me make my own bed and help with the dishes before I was allowed to go and ride the horses around the estate. It was this experience that led me to be able to be an ordinary woman in ordinary circumstances. And to her I owe this Oscar. To the Dragon Lady, Auntie May.

The Book

Through the window he could see the old man sitting in an intricately carved chair, feet up on the grand oak desk and reading what looked to be a first edition, leather bound book. He pushed open the heavy, glazed door into the curiosity shop and made his way through the tables laden with bric-a-brac, porcelain figurines, delicate china tableware, mirrors, clocks, scientific instruments and unidentifiable objects. The dim light struggled through the air, catching at dust motes in the weak candle glow.

He had identified, on an earlier visit, what he actually wanted to buy. It was a rare glass receptacle, ideal for his next experiment. It was no longer on show, so the old man must have moved it into an even darker, more obscure space, presumably to remove it from further interest.

On spying him, the old man rose creakily from his chair, raised a feeble hand, and moved unsteadily to the back of the shop, to a space behind a dusty curtain and in so doing, disappeared from view.

The younger man took the seat thus vacated. He picked up the book that the old man had abandoned and began reading.

...and the bombs crashed around their heads as they scrambled through the sucking, squelching mud, trying to gain a place of safety. A giant crater needed to be negotiated. George volunteered to hold the pursuers off while the others made a path around it.

Standing behind a blasted tree, George aimed his rifle into the flashing darkness, shouting over the din, 'Just get a move on, I can't wait here for ever'.

They forged a path through the debris of the attack, trying not to think too hard about it, until they were around the crater and close to the remains of a shattered building.

'We can hold it now, George,' shouted Tim. 'Keep your head down and make your way over here'.

George carefully followed the path made by his comrades and almost made it, but a singing whistle spat, and George called, 'I'm hit!'

He staggered, but kept forging forwards, clutching his arm. The bullet wound didn't seem fatal, but he could no longer hold the rifle. He dropped it, and lunged forward the last few yards into the waiting arms of his friends.

They helped him into the shelter that Alf had located and found that it was an abandoned enemy stronghold, complete with short-wave radio. They called in their location and did their best to clean and dress George's wound.

As they waited for the bombardment to ease, each man refusing to admit his terror, they looked around for food, for water. Tim called excitedly that he had found a bottle of gin. Alf said that all he had found was a book. Tim poured out the gin into the last remaining undamaged cups, and Alf gave the book to George.

'Here, this'll pass the time while we wait for rescue. George, read it to us. It'll take your mind off your arm.' George nodded grimly and began...

She sank into the rocking chair and sighed a sigh of pleasure. This afternoon had been more than she had hoped for. With her husband away, and the children in school, she had taken a taxi to the Grand Hotel to meet Jason, for the third time. This time, she had put on her special underthings, and her most careful make-up. With her best perfume and the earrings John had bought for her birthday, she felt truly wicked, and excited beyond endurance.

Jason was there before her. He had a bottle of champagne on ice, and a light lunch ordered for after. After. It was the 'after' that the meeting was about. She had lusted after Jason ever since the party at Evie's, when he had charmed her with his smile, his light humour and his oh-so-sexy smile.

He greeted her with a playful bow; whispered into her ear that he was glad she had decided to join him, and wondered if she might like to drink the champagne in the room he had booked. Of course she did. Her life with a businessman, a mortgage, two children, and fourteen days a year in a time share in the Algarve needed all the help it could get. And help it got.

Jason was everything she had hoped. Gentle, romantic, insistent, exploratory, imaginative and tireless. Some hours later, the champagne drunk, the lunch room-serviced and the underthings replaced, Jason called her a taxi and they arranged to meet the following week.

She arrived home just as the nanny was bringing the children in from school. Stretching luxuriously, she rose from the rocking chair, ready to greet her real life. Nanny opened the front door and the children rushed in, full of the news of their day as the grandfather clock chimed four. She listened patiently to tales of circle time, friends' squabbles, teacher's pleasure with a test result but just wanted to calm them so that her whirling emotions could settle.

'Would you like me to read you a story?' she asked. Of course they said yes, so she opened their favourite book and began.

Mamma Bear and Baby Bear went down into the wood.
'Mamma Bear,' said Baby Bear, 'I wonder if I could
Go down the road between the trees and on until the house
Where Uncle Bear and Cousin Bear have kept a little mouse?'
'You can,' she said, 'but please take care
You don't see nasty humans there.
For they are known to take young bears
And put them in big chains and snares
And keep them in cold cages too.
I don't want that to happen to you.'

'We will take care, dear Mamma Bear
We won't see nasty humans there
And if we do, we promise you,
We know exactly what to do.
We must tell a grown up bear
Who will chase the human over there
And eat him up and take his chains
And all his cages so he gains
Nothing by bothering us bears
And giving us such woes and cares'.

And off they went, to find their cousin
And friends and pals by the dozen.
But suddenly, to their surprise,
Down the hill, before their eyes
There was a man, a human being
Looking around him, and never seeing
The baby bears coming lower and lower

He forgot he was on a motor lawnmower.
It ran amok, into the trees
He struggled with his hands and knees
To stop the mower, to get it to halt.
The erratic swerving made the bears bolt.
And back they went to Mamma Bear.
They'd gone as far as they might dare.

And Mamma Bear was so delighted
That they had been a little frighted
So would take care another day
Without the need to run away.

She closed the book and put it on the table. She never really understood why the children loved this particular book; it never failed to make them laugh. But it meant something. Was it a warning from the universe to take more care? She didn't know, but it was certainly something to think about. At that point, she heard a key in the door...

George paused in his reading. They could hear, now the shelling and bombing had eased, a vehicle coming their way. Alf, at the door, waved that it was an ambulance come to get George. Well, it seemed they had survived this one. But at that moment...

He heard the old man shuffling back from behind the curtain. He put down the book and took the box, handing the money to the old man. He made his way carefully through the cramped space and back out into the open air.

Blessings of the Gods

The thunder boomed and the lightning flashed, reflecting brokenly in the swirling, furious waves, as the two great gods fought out yet another of their brotherly disagreements. Caught between the anger of Poseidon and the violence of Zeus, the fragile boat tore apart, and only one sailor was washed upon the beach.

Wet, cold and terrified, he scrambled up the shore and onto a grassy field. Ahead of him was a small, controlled fire and a beautiful young woman who invited him to join her. She could see he was in need of food, of drink, of warmth, and clothing. She provided all of these, for she was indeed a goddess. But beyond that, for she was Demeter, goddess of the harvest, she showed him her deepest secret, because she loved him.

She showed him how to take the seeds from the grasses, how to press them into powder, mix them with oil and water and put to bake on the hot stones surrounding the fire. Zeus was angry with her and stole her daughter, to punish her. But he did not punish the man, for the fault was not his.

On another part of the island, the sun burned down and scorched the earth, as Apollo drew his chariot too close to the land. Parched and starving, for the food was all burned, a young man sought shelter from the burning air.

A hand beckoned him from a thicket, as yet untouched by the heat. A beautiful young woman called him in, for she had taken pity on this stranger. At that moment, a boar ran past, and somehow fell to her spear, because she was Artemis, goddess of hunting. She cooked the boar and offered the meat to the stranger. He ate his fill, but was unable to consume it all. He wanted to offer the remains to the gods, but she told him instead, how to preserve the remains, so that he could carry it and not need to hunt every day. For giving away a secret of the gods, Zeus punished her, by making her kill the one she loved. But the man was innocent, so went free.

On yet another part of the island, a young woman, fleeing from a cruel shepherd, was crawling, exhausted, through the mud as the rain beat down upon her back. Before her, just visible through the falling tempest, she could see a herd of resplendent cattle. She approached the nearest cow, a beautiful black and white, large, patient animal and asked if she might have some milk.

The cow was happy to let her suckle sustenance, because the cow belonged to Aristaeus, god of pastoral farming, and dairy husbandry. Aristaeus saw her need, and lent her a receptacle to collect the milk. But there was no lid, so she could not take the milk with her on her journey. Accordingly, because he saw her need, Aristaeus taught her a godly method of preserving milk so it could be carried. He showed her how to shake the milk until it became solid. Zeus was furious and sent thunderbolts which killed many of Aristaeus' hives. But he did not punish the young woman, for she was modest, and only asked for milk to drink.

The three met. They shared their gifts, showing each other what they had been taught by the gods and amalgamated their prizes. And as the humans worked together to combine their new-found methods into new forms, the sun shone warmly; Notus, the south wind blew gentle breezes to surround them; Chloris made flowers grow; and sweet water flowed by grace of the naiads. For these spirits recognised that the three blessed humans were the benefactors of all mankind, for all time.

And there was consternation on Olympia, as the gods realised they had been overcome. That they would no longer be able to rely on offerings; that they would, in time, cease to matter. By sharing simple gifts, they had given away secrets to the human race. These puny humans would win, they would proliferate and rule the earth, the seas and the skies. The baker, the butcher and the dairyman had joined the gifts given freely in friendship and had created something even the greatest of the gods had failed to do. They had made a bacon sandwich.

Ladies Who Lunch

The ladies had had a lovely morning in Westwood Cross. They had bought clothes in Primark, flavoured oils upstairs in T K Maxx, a nice little treat for later in Marks. And now they were enjoying lunch. Lucy and Gabi were sitting in the rather pleasant café upstairs in Debenhams. Gabi had a light lemon cous cous with a green side salad, but Lucy was taking the opportunity of the steak and ale pie with chips and gravy. On the next table was a young woman with a toddler.

They were discussing the art exhibition which was the culmination of the year's art group's efforts. They had both put several pieces in, and both had sold a couple.

'I can't believe someone actually wanted to buy two of my paintings,' said Gabi, 'I think I have improved, but it was such a shock.'

'Nonsense', countered Lucy. 'Your paintings are excellent. I'm only surprised that you didn't sell more. I really think that one of the ducks would have gone. And the portrait of the kitten.'

'Yes', I must admit, I am proud of that one', admitted Gabi.

Lucy made a note in her book.

'And on the subject of buying' said Gabi, changing the subject, although she claimed she wasn't, 'what was all that about bargaining with that man outside? You do know that he is probably struggling with money, and is only selling his craft to feed his kids?'

'That's not the point,' argued Lucy, 'He was asking £19.99 for it. A hand-made toy. It was nice, but not worth twenty quid'

'Possibly not, but that's not the point. He clearly needs the twenty pounds, and was offering all he had.'

'I might have paid fifteen, but I think he was pushing it with twenty'.

'Then why didn't you pay fifteen? Why did you have to bargain him all the way down to ten. It probably cost him that to make it. You could have been a bit more charitable. It was just greed'.

'But I did get it for ten, so I suppose I win'.

Lucy made a note in her book.

'Did you hear back from that man you were chatting up last week?'

'Yes, I did,' said Gabi, cautiously. 'He asked to meet me again.

'Wow,' replied Lucy. 'And are you going to meet him? He really was attractive. We don't get many chances like that at our age. I certainly would.'

'Don't be ridiculous,' snapped Gabi, 'I am a married woman.'

Gabi made a note in her book.

'Do you want a pudding?' asked Lucy. 'The chocolate cake looks wonderful.'

'I don't know,' pondered Gabi. 'I quite like the look of the cream scones. Or the lemon drizzle cake.'

'And that ginger slice looks so moist and heavy. Oh, I don't know. Why don't we get a selection and share? One of each, that way we don't have to choose.'

'It's a good idea, shall I go over and ask if we can have a selection of smaller pieces?'

'Good idea. But why go for smaller pieces? You've only had a salad. You can afford some cake.'

But their conversation was distracted by the toddler on the next table who chose that moment to throw a tantrum. His mother tried to calm him. She tried to entertain him. She tried to offer him food. She tried everything but he was not to be stopped.

'If you are going to look at the cake, you can go and have a word with her about that kid. She should take him out, disturbing people like that. Children and mothers like that make me so angry.'

Gabi did. She approached the mother.

'Let me take him for a few minutes,' she offered.

Gabi took him to the window and started pointing out things in the shopping centre. Patiently, she calmed him, played with him and cheered him. Then she took him to the counter and bought him a packet of sweeties and his mother a cup of tea.

Lucy made a note in Gabi's book.

When Gabi got back, she said that she had decided against the cake. She didn't really want a lot and couldn't choose anyway.

Lucy reluctantly made another note in Gabi's book.

114

'While I was gone, you could have tidied up the table,' accused Gabi.

'Why?' asked Lucy. It's not my job. Those women over there are paid to do it. Why should I do their work? Anyway, if everyone did it, they'd be out of employment.'

'Don't be silly. It's just laziness. They are rushed off their feet. It wouldn't have taken much effort to take the tray to the counter.'

'Well, I didn't.'

And with that, a woman cleared and wiped the table.

Lucy made a note in her own book.

'Well, that's pretty much it for today,' announced Gabi suddenly. 'But before we leave, I am going to get that nice jacket over there. Will you stay here with the bags while I go, please?'

When she got to the rack, she was disappointed to see that there was only one in her size and another woman was wearing it, trying it on. And it looked superb on her.

'I wanted that,' Gabi said.

'Oh, sorry,' replied the woman. 'Let me just try it on for a couple of minutes. I'm looking for something for my daughter's wedding. What do you think?'

Gabi thought that the woman looked much better in it than she would. She was envious of how nice the woman looked, and was tempted to tell her the colour was wrong.

But instead, she said, 'It looks wonderful on you. Please take it, I can look for something else'.

The mark went in Gabi's book.

The lunch was over and Lucy and Gabi stood to leave. As the two nice ladies continued their gossip, Lucy and Gabi made their way to the escalators.

'Do you actually like doing this?' asked Gabi.

'Yeah, sure, why not? Taking over unsuspecting humans and tempting them. It's easy work and can be fun, although to be fair, these two were a bit dull.

'How do you think that one went?'

'Ah, it was okay, but I think game to you this time, 4-3, Gab. I got pride, avarice and sloth. You got lust, gluttony, wrath and envy. How are we on aggregate?'

'Depends what you're counting,' said Gabi. 'I think I'm ahead on games, but you on points.'

'How does that work?'

'Well, I've won more games, I think, but when you win, it's always a bigger margin. You know, my wins tend to be 4-3, but yours are more often 5-2 or even 6-1.'

'Yeah, makes sense. What do you want to do tomorrow? Married couple?'

'No, I don't like doing married couples. I always find the lust a bit awkward. What about Tesco Extra check out? I could be on the till and you could be the customer.'

Gabi wasn't sure. 'I don't know, I don't think there's enough wiggle room. How will we manage patience? I tell you what, we haven't done A&E for ages.

'Oh, yes! I like A&E. Staff or patients?'

'If I remember correctly, we did staff last time. Let's do patients.'

'Ok. It's a date. QEQM it is.'

And with that, they parted. Gabriel went to the up escalator. Took off his jacket, shook his wings out and let his halo sparkle, just a bit, as he entered into the light. Lucifer, on the down escalator, stretched his goat's legs, swished his tale and grinned as his horns gleamed redly in the approaching darkness.

www.ingramcontent.com/pod-product-compliance
Lightning Source LLC
Chambersburg PA
CBHW021927170626
46807CB00007B/3014